SCOTTISH FOLK AND FAIRY TALES

> *Do you believe in fairies? . . . If you*
> *believe, clap your hands.*

J. M. Barrie, *Peter Pan*

When I was asked to edit this collection of classic Scottish folk tales and fairy tales, I jumped at the opportunity. What a wonderful wealth of source ma_____ ___ose from, I thought! And so it has amply proved. _____ _____ I could find – stories like 'Tam L___ _____ _____ old Border ballads of the 14th ___ ____ _____ like 'Adam Bell', taken from th_ _____ _____; Burns' epic folk-tale 'Tam O' _____'; _____ _____ the work of those industrious _____ ___ Scott and Robert Chambers in Edinburgh ___ _____ J. F. Campbell in the Gaelic-speaking part of the West Highlands and the Hebrides; and here are stories by great Victorian and 20th-century writers.

It is a real pleasure to reprint Andrew Lang's story 'The Gold of Fairnilee', which has been described – rightly, I think – as one of the finest of all the Victorian fairy tales. It is interesting to note the historical background to this story – the horrors of a war on your own doorstep – whose action was triggered off by the battle of Flodden in 1513. Watch out in this magic narrative for the ingenious explanation of Tam Hislop's seven-year disappearance on the eve of the battle, not to Fairyland at all, as Hislop told his neighbours, but a simple deserter hiding out at Perth from the perils of Border warfare. Note too how the action in James Hogg's story 'Adam Bell' commences with the disappearance of the main character 'on the very day that Prince Charles Stuart defeated General Hawley on Falkirk Muir' in that other momentous year – 1745. I suspect that supernatural stories flourish best in periods of civil strife, of which Scotland has had more than its share. And I'm sure that if I had lived at the time of Flodden, I too would have been very tempted to do a seven-year disappearing trick rather than get dragged into one of their suicidal wars.

It is good __ ____ ____ ___ _____ __ _____ __ _ time when

Scottish schools are being urged to introduce Scottish writing and culture from an early age. 'Scottish texts should be actively sought and used in class-rooms . . . they should permeate the curriculum and be introduced from an early stage', urges a current document. I commend these stories to that new generation of readers in particular.

Gordon Jarvie

Other selections from Gordon Jarvie

IRISH FOLK AND FAIRY TALES
THE GENIUS AND OTHER IRISH STORIES

SCOTTISH FOLK AND FAIRY TALES

Chosen and edited by
GORDON JARVIE

Illustrated by
BARBARA BROWN

PUFFIN BOOKS

PUFFIN BOOKS

Published by the Penguin Group
Penguin Books Ltd, 27 Wrights Lane, London W8 5TZ, England
Penguin Books USA Inc., 375 Hudson Street, New York, New York 10014, USA
Penguin Books Australia Ltd, Ringwood, Victoria, Australia
Penguin Books Canada Ltd, 10 Alcorn Avenue, Toronto, Ontario, Canada M4V 3B2
Penguin Books (NZ) Ltd, 182–190 Wairau Road, Auckland 10, New Zealand

Penguin Books Ltd, Registered Offices: Harmondsworth, Middlesex, England

First published 1992
3 5 7 9 10 8 6 4 2

Grateful acknowledgement is made to John Lorne Campbell of Canna for
permission to quote the story 'Why Everyone Should be Able to Tell a Story';
and to David Higham Associates for permission to quote the story 'The Lonely Giant', by
Alasdair MacLean, from *The Noel Streatfeild Holiday Book*

Filmset in Monophoto Sabon
Printed in England by Clays Ltd, St Ives plc

CONTENTS

PART ONE:

MAGIC-LORE

The Milk-white Doo   *Elizabeth Grierson*   9
The Well o' the World's End   *Elizabeth Grierson*   15
The Seal Catcher and the Merman
    Elizabeth Grierson   20
The Laird of Morphie and the Water Kelpie
    Elizabeth Grierson   27
The Laird o' Co   *Elizabeth Grierson*   32
The Brownie o' Ferne-Den   *Elizabeth Grierson*   37
Katherine Crackernuts   *Elizabeth Grierson*   43
Tam Lin   *Traditional*   54
Thomas Rymer   *Traditional*   60
Gold-tree and Silver-tree   *Joseph Jacobs*   65
The Magic Walking-stick   *John Buchan*   70

PART TWO:

GIANTS AND MONSTERS

The Two Shepherds   *J. F. Campbell*   87
The Sprightly Tailor   *Joseph Jacobs*   90
The Lonely Giant   *Alasdair MacLean*   94
Assipattle and the Mester Stoorworm
    Elizabeth Grierson   106

PART THREE:

APPARITIONS, SECOND SIGHT AND WITCHES

Adam Bell   *James Hogg*   125
The Grey Wolf   *George MacDonald*   132
Through the Veil   *Sir Arthur Conan Doyle*   140

Contents

PART FOUR:
A CLASSIC VICTORIAN FAIRY TALE

The Gold of Fairnilee   *Andrew Lang*   149

PART FIVE:
ENVOY

Why Everyone Should be Able to Tell a Story
   John Lorne Campbell   197
The Tail   *J. F. Campbell*   199

Part One

MAGIC-LORE

THE MILK-WHITE DOO

Elizabeth Grierson

There was once a man who got his living by working in the fields. He had one little son, called Curly-locks, and one little daughter, called Golden-tresses; but his wife was dead, and, as he had to be out all day, these children were often left alone. So, as he was afraid that some evil might befall them when there was no one to look after them, he, in an ill day, married again.

I say 'in an ill day', for his second wife was a most deceitful woman, who really hated children, although she pretended, before her marriage, to love them. And she was so unkind to them, and made the house so uncomfortable with her bad temper, that her poor husband often sighed to himself, and wished that he had let well alone, and remained a widower.

But it was no use crying over spilt milk; the deed was done, and he had just to try to make the best of it. So things went on for several years, until the children were beginning to run about out of doors and play by themselves.

Then one day the Goodman chanced to catch a hare, and

he brought it home and gave it to his wife to cook for the dinner.

Now his wife was a very good cook, and she made the hare into a pot of delicious soup; but she was also very greedy, and while the soup was boiling she tasted it, and tasted it, till at last she discovered that it was almost gone. Then she was in a fine state of mind, for she knew that her husband would soon be coming home for his dinner, and that she would have nothing to set before him.

So what do you think the wicked woman did? She went out to the door, where her little stepson, Curly-locks, was playing in the sun, and told him to come in and get his face washed. And while she was washing his face, she struck him on the head with a hammer and stunned him, and popped him into the pot to make soup for his father's dinner.

By and by the Goodman came in from his work, and the soup was dished up; and he, and his wife, and his little daughter, Golden-tresses, sat down to sup it.

'Where's Curly-locks?' asked the Goodman. 'It's a pity he is not here while the soup is hot.'

'How should I ken where he is?' answered his wife crossly. 'I have other work to do than to run about after a mischievous laddie all the morning.'

The Goodman went on supping his soup in silence for some minutes; then he lifted up a little foot in his spoon.

'This is Curly-locks' foot,' he cried in horror. 'There's been ill work here.'

'Hoots, havers,' answered his wife, laughing, pretending to be very much amused. 'What should Curly-locks' foot be doing in the soup? 'Tis the hare's forefoot, which is very like that of a bairn.'

But presently the Goodman took something else up in his spoon.

'This is Curly-locks' hand,' he said shrilly. 'I ken it by the crook in its little finger.'

'The man's demented,' retorted his wife, 'not to ken the hind foot of a hare when he sees it!'

So the poor father did not say any more, but went away back to his work, sorely perplexed in his mind; while his little daughter, Golden-tresses, who had a shrewd suspicion of what had happened, gathered all the bones from the empty plates, and, carrying them away in her apron, buried them beneath a flat stone, close by a white rose tree that grew by the cottage door.

And, lo and behold! those poor bones, which she buried with such care –

> '*Grew and grew,*
> *To a milk-white Doo,*
> *That took its wings,*
> *And away it flew.*'

And at last it lighted on a tuft of grass by a burnside, where two women were washing clothes. It sat there cooing to itself for some time; then it sang this song softly to them:

> '*Pew, pew,*
> *My mimmie me slew,*
> *My daddy me chew,*
> *My sister gathered my banes,*
> *And put them between two milk-white stanes.*
> *And I grew and grew*
> *To a milk-white Doo,*
> *And I took to my wings and away I flew.*'

The women stopped washing and looked at one another in astonishment. It was not every day that they came across a bird that could sing a song like that, and they felt that there was something not canny about it.

'Sing that song again, my bonnie bird,' said one of them at last, 'and we'll give you all these clothes!'

So the bird sang its song over again, and the washerwomen gave it all the clothes, and it tucked them under its right wing, and flew on.

Presently it came to a house where all the windows were open, and it perched on one of the window-sills, and inside it saw a man counting out a great heap of silver.

And, sitting on the window-sill, it sang its song to him:

> 'Pew, pew,
> My mimmie me slew,
> My daddy me chew,
> My sister gathered my banes,
> And put them between two milk-white stanes.
> And I grew and grew
> To a milk-white Doo,
> And I took to my wings and away I flew.'

The man stopped counting his silver, and listened. He felt, like the washerwomen, that there was something not canny about this Doo. When it had finished its song, he said:

'Sing that song again, my bonnie bird, and I'll give you a' this siller in a bag.'

So the Doo sang its song over again, and got the bag of silver, which it tucked under its left wing. Then it flew on.

It had not flown very far, however, before it came to a mill where two millers were grinding corn. And it settled down on a sack of meal and sang its song to them.

> 'Pew, pew,
> My mimmie me slew,
> My daddy me chew,
> My sister gathered my banes,

And put them between two milk-white stanes.
And I grew and grew
To a milk-white Doo,
And I took to my wings and away I flew.'

The millers stopped their work, and looked at one another, scratching their heads in amazement.

'Sing that song over again, my bonnie bird!' exclaimed
both of them together when the Doo had finished, 'and we
will give you this millstone.'

So the Doo repeated its song, and got the millstone,
which it asked one of the millers to lift on to its back; then it
flew out of the mill, and up the valley, leaving the two men
staring after it dumb with astonishment.

As you may think, the milk-white Doo had a heavy load
to carry, but it went bravely on till it came within sight of
its father's cottage, and lighted down at last on the thatched
roof.

Then it laid its burdens on the thatch, and, flying down to

the courtyard, picked up a number of little chuckie stones. With them in its beak it flew back to the roof, and began to throw them down the chimney.

By this time it was evening, and the Goodman and his wife, and his little daughter, Golden-tresses, were sitting round the table eating their supper. And you may be sure that they were all very much startled when the stones came rattling down the chimney, bringing such a cloud of soot with them that they were almost smothered. They all jumped up from their chairs, and ran outside to see what the matter was.

And Golden-tresses, being the littlest, ran the fastest, and when she came out at the door the milk-white Doo flung the bundle of clothes down at her feet.

And the father came out next, and the milk-white Doo flung the bag of silver down at his feet.

But the wicked stepmother, being somewhat stout, came out last, and the milk-white Doo threw the millstone right down on her head and killed her.

Then it spread its wings and flew away, and has never been seen again; but it had made the Goodman and his daughter rich for life, and it had rid them of the cruel stepmother, so that they lived in peace and plenty for the remainder of their days.

THE WELL O' THE WORLD'S END

Elizabeth Grierson

There was once an old widow woman, who lived in a little cottage with her only daughter, who was such a bonnie lassie that everyone liked to look at her.

One day the old woman took a notion into her head to bake a girdleful of cakes. So she took down her baking-board, and went to the meal-chest and fetched a basinful of meal; but when she went to seek a jug of water to mix the meal with, she found that there was none in the house.

So she called to her daughter, who was in the garden; and when the girl came she held out the empty jug to her, saying, 'Run, like a good lassie, to the Well o' the World's End and bring me a jug of water, for I have long found that water from the Well o' the World's End makes the best cakes.'

So the lassie took the jug and set out on her errand.

Now, as its name shows, it is a long road to that well, and

many a weary mile had the poor maid to go ere she reached it.

But she arrived there at last; and what was her disappointment to find it dry.

She was so tired and so vexed that she sat down beside it and began to cry; for she did not know where to get any more water, and she felt that she could not go back to her mother with an empty jug.

While she was crying, a nice yellow paddock, with very bright eyes, came jump-jump-jumping over the stones of the well, and squatted down at her feet, looking up into her face.

'And why are ye crying, my bonnie maid?' he asked. 'Is there anything I can do to help you?'

'I am crying because the well is empty,' she answered, 'and I cannot get any water to carry home to my mother.'

'Listen,' said the paddock softly. 'I can get you water in plenty, if you'll promise to be my wife.'

Now the lassie had but one thought in her head, and that was to get the water for her mother's oatcakes, and she never for a moment thought that the paddock was serious, so she promised gladly enough to be his wife, if he would just get her a jug of water.

No sooner had the words passed her lips than the beastie jumped down the mouth of the well, and in another moment it was full to the brim with water.

The lassie filled her jug and carried it home, without troubling any more about the matter. But late that night, just as her mother and she were going to bed, something came with a faint 'thud, thud' against the cottage door, and then they heard a tiny little wee voice singing:

> '*Oh, open the door, my hinnie, my heart,*
> *Oh, open the door, my ain true love;*
> *Remember the promise that you and I made*
> *Down i' the meadow, where we two met.*'

'Wheesht,' said the old woman, raising her head. 'What noise is that at the door?'

'Oh,' said her daughter, who was feeling rather frightened, 'it's only a yellow paddock.'

'Poor bit beastie,' said the kind-hearted old mother. 'Open the door and let him in. It's cold work sitting on the doorstep.'

So the lassie, very unwillingly, opened the door, and the paddock came jump-jump-jumping across the kitchen, and sat down at the fireside.

And while he sat there he began to sing this song:

> '*Oh, gie me my supper, my hinnie, my heart,*
> *Oh, gie me my supper, my ain true love;*
> *Remember the promise that you and I made*
> *Down i' the meadow, where we two met.*'

'Gie the poor beast his supper,' said the old woman. 'He's an uncommon paddock that can sing like that.'

'Tut,' replied her daughter crossly, for she was growing more and more frightened as she saw the creature's bright black eyes fixed on her face. 'I'm not going to be so silly as to feed a wet, sticky paddock.'

'Don't be ill-natured and cruel,' said her mother. 'Who knows how far the little beastie has travelled? And I warrant that it would like a saucerful of milk.'

Now, the lassie could have told her that the paddock had travelled from the Well o' the World's End; but she held her tongue, and went into the pantry, and brought back a saucerful of milk, which she set down before the strange little visitor.

> '*Now chap off my head, my hinnie, my heart,*
> *Now chap off my head, my ain true love,*
> *Remember the promise that you and I made*
> *Down i' the meadow, where we two met.*'

'Hout, havers, pay no heed, the creature's daft,' exclaimed the old woman, running forward to stop her daughter, who was raising the axe to chop off the paddock's head. But she was too late; down came the axe, off went the head; and, lo and behold! on the spot where the little creature had sat, stood the handsomest young Prince that had ever been seen.

He wore such a noble air, and was so richly dressed, that the astonished girl and her mother would have fallen on their knees before him had he not prevented them by a movement of his hand.

'It is I that should kneel to you, Sweetheart,' he said, turning to the blushing girl, 'for you have delivered me from a fearful spell, which was cast over me in my infancy by a wicked fairy, who at the same time slew my father. For long years I have lived in that well, the Well o' the World's End, waiting for a maiden to appear, who should take pity on me, even in my loathsome disguise, and promise to be my wife – a maiden who would also have the kindness to let me into her house, and the courage, at my bidding, to cut off my head.

'Now I can return and claim my father's kingdom, and you, most gracious maiden, will go with me, and be my bride, if you will have me.'

And this was how the lassie who went to fetch water from the Well o' the World's End became a princess.

THE SEAL CATCHER AND
THE MERMAN

Elizabeth Grierson

Once upon a time there was a man who lived not very far from John-o'-Groat's House, which, as everyone knows, is in the far north of Scotland. He lived in a little cottage by the sea-shore, and made his living by catching seals and selling their fur, which in those days was very valuable.

He earned a good deal of money in this way, for these creatures used to come out of the sea in large numbers, and lie on the rocks near his house basking in the sunshine, so that it was not difficult to creep up behind them and kill them.

Some of those seals were larger than others, and the country people used to call them 'Roane', and whisper that they were not seals at all, but mermen and merwomen, who came from a country of their own, far down under the ocean, who assumed this strange disguise in order that they might pass through the water, and come up to breathe the air of this earth of ours.

But the seal catcher only laughed at them, and said that

20

those seals were most worth killing, for their skins were so big that he got an extra price for them.

Now it chanced one day, when he was pursuing his calling, that he stabbed a seal with his hunting-knife, and whether the stroke had not been sure enough or not, I cannot say, but with a loud cry of pain the creature slipped off the rock into the sea, and disappeared under the water, carrying the knife along with it.

The seal catcher, much annoyed at his clumsiness, and also at the loss of his knife, went home to dinner in a very downcast frame of mind. On his way he met a horseman, who was so tall and so strange-looking, and who rode on such a gigantic horse, that he stopped and looked at him in astonishment, wondering who he was, and from what country he came.

The stranger stopped also, and asked him his trade, and on hearing that he was a seal catcher, he immediately ordered a great number of seal skins. The seal catcher was delighted, for such an order meant a large sum of money to him. But his face fell when the horseman added that it was absolutely necessary that the skins should be delivered that evening.

'I cannot do it,' he said, in a disappointed voice, 'for the seals will not come back to the rocks again until tomorrow morning.'

'I can take you to a place where there are any number of seals,' answered the stranger, 'if you will mount behind me on my horse and come with me.'

The seal catcher agreed to this, and climbed up behind the rider, who shook his bridle rein, and off the great horse galloped at such a pace that he had much ado to keep his seat.

On and on they went, flying like the wind, until at last they came to the edge of a huge precipice, the face of which went sheer down to the sea. Here the mysterious horseman pulled up his steed with a jerk.

'Get off now,' he said shortly.

The seal catcher did as he was bid, and when he found himself safe on the ground, he peeped cautiously over the edge of the cliff, to see if there were any seals lying on the rocks below.

To his astonishment he saw below him no rocks, only the blue sea, which came right up to the foot of the cliff.

'Where are the seals that you spoke of?' he asked anxiously, wishing that he had never set out on such a rash adventure.

'You will see presently,' answered the stranger, who was attending to his horse's bridle.

The seal catcher was now thoroughly frightened, for he felt sure that some evil was about to befall him, and in such a lonely place he knew that it would be useless to cry out for help.

And it seemed as if his fears would prove only too true, for the next moment the stranger's hand was laid upon his shoulder, and he felt himself being hurled bodily over the cliff, and then he fell with a splash into the sea.

He thought that his last hour had come, and he wondered how anyone could commit such a wrong deed upon an innocent man.

But, to his astonishment, he found that some change must have come over him, for instead of being choked by the water, he could breathe quite easily, and he and his companion, who was still close at his side, seemed to be sinking as quickly down through the sea as they had flown through the air.

Down and down they went, nobody knows how far, till at last they came to a huge arched door, which appeared to be made of pink coral, studded over with cockle-shells. It opened, of its own accord, and when they entered they found themselves in a huge hall, the walls of which were formed of mother-of-pearl, and the floor of which was of sea-sand, smooth, and firm, and yellow.

The hall was crowded with occupants, but they were seals, not men, and when the seal catcher turned to his companion to ask him what it all meant, he was aghast to find that he, too, had assumed the form of a seal. He was still more aghast when he caught sight of himself in a large mirror that hung on the wall, and saw that he also no longer bore the likeness of a man, but was transformed into a nice, hairy, brown seal.

'Ah, woe is me,' he said to himself, 'through no fault of mine this artful stranger has laid some baneful charm upon me, and in this awful guise will I remain for the rest of my natural life.'

At first none of the huge creatures spoke to him. For some reason or other they seemed to be very sad, and moved gently about the hall, talking quietly and mournfully to one another, or lay sadly upon the sandy floor, wiping big tears from their eyes with their soft furry fins.

But presently they began to notice him, and to whisper to

23

one another, and presently his guide moved away from him, and disappeared through a door at the end of the hall. When he returned he held a huge knife in his hand.

'Did you ever see this before?' he asked, holding it out to the unfortunate seal catcher, who, to his horror, recognized his own hunting-knife with which he had struck the seal in the morning, and which had been carried off by the wounded animal.

At the sight of it he fell upon his face and begged for mercy, for he at once came to the conclusion that the inhabitants of the cavern, enraged at the harm which had been wrought upon their comrade, had, in some magic way, contrived to capture him, and to bring him down to their subterranean abode, in order to work their vengeance upon him by killing him.

But, instead of doing so, they crowded round him, rubbing their soft noses against his fur to show their sympathy, and implored him not to be afraid, for no harm would befall him, and they would love him all their lives long if he would only do what they asked him.

'Tell me what you ask,' said the seal catcher, 'and I will do it, if it lies within my power.'

'Follow me,' answered his guide, and he led the way to the door through which he had disappeared when he went to seek the knife.

The seal catcher followed him. And there, in a smaller room, he found a great brown seal lying on a bed of pale pink seaweed, with a gaping wound in his side.

'That is my father,' said his guide, 'whom you wounded this morning, thinking that he was one of the common seals who live in the sea, instead of a merman who has speech, and understanding, as you mortals have. I brought you here to bind up his wounds, for no other hand than yours can heal him.'

'I have no skill in the art of healing,' said the seal catcher, astonished at the forbearance of these strange creatures, whom he had so unwittingly wronged; 'but I will bind up the wound to the best of my power, and I am only sorry that it was my hands that caused it.'

He went over to the bed, and, stooping over the wounded merman, washed and dressed the hurt as well as he could; and the touch of his hands appeared to work like magic, for no sooner had he finished than the wound seemed to deaden and die, leaving only a scar, and the old seal sprang up, as well as ever.

Then there was great rejoicing throughout the whole Palace of the Seals. They laughed, and they talked, and they embraced each other in their own strange way, crowding round their comrade, and rubbing their noses against his, as if to show him how delighted they were at his recovery.

But all this while the seal catcher stood alone in a corner, with his mind filled with dark thoughts, for although he saw now that they had no intention of killing him, he did not relish the prospect of spending the rest of his life in the guise of a seal, fathoms deep under the ocean.

But presently, to his great joy, his guide approached him, and said, 'Now you are at liberty to return home to your wife and children. I will take you to them, but only on one condition.'

'And what is that?' asked the seal catcher eagerly, overjoyed at the prospect of being restored safely to the upper world, and to his family.

'That you will take a solemn oath never to wound a seal again.'

'That will I do right gladly,' the seal catcher replied, for although the promise meant giving up his means of livelihood, he felt that if only he regained his proper shape he could always turn his hand to something else.

So he took the required oath with all due solemnity, holding up his fin as he swore, and all the other seals crowded round him as witnesses. And a sigh of relief went through the halls when the words were spoken, for he was the most famous seal catcher in the North.

Then he bade the strange company farewell, and, accompanied by his guide, passed once more through the outer doors of coral, and up, and up, and up, through the shadowy green water, until it began to grow lighter and lighter, and at last they emerged into the sunshine of earth.

Then, with one spring, they reached the top of the cliff, where the great black horse was waiting for them, quietly nibbling the green turf.

When they left the water their strange disguise dropped from them, and they were now as they had been before, a plain seal catcher and a tall, well-dressed gentleman in riding clothes.

'Get up behind me,' said the latter, as he swung himself into his saddle. The seal catcher did as he was bid, taking tight hold of his companion's coat, for he remembered how nearly he had fallen off on his previous journey.

Then it all happened as it happened before. The bridle was shaken, and the horse galloped off, and it was not long before the seal catcher found himself standing in safety before his own garden gate.

He held out his hand to say 'goodbye', but as he did so the stranger pulled out a huge bag of gold and placed it in it.

'You've done your part of the bargain – we must do ours,' he said. 'Men shall never say that we took away an honest man's work without giving him some compensation for it, and here is what will keep you in comfort to your life's end.'

Then he vanished, and when the astonished seal catcher carried the bag into his cottage, and turned the gold out on the table, he found that what the stranger had said was true, and that he would be a rich man for the remainder of his days.

THE LAIRD OF MORPHIE AND THE WATER KELPIE

Elizabeth Grierson

There was once a Scottish laird whose name was Graham of Morphie, and, as he was rich and great, he determined to build himself a grand castle. But, besides being rich, he was somewhat miserly, and he did not like the thought of having to pay a great deal of money for the building of it. So he hit on a plan by which he thought he could get labour cheaply. And this was the plan.

Down in the valley, close to where he lived, there was a large deep loch, and in the loch, so the country folk said, there dwelt a water kelpie.

Now water kelpies, as all the world knows, are cruel and malicious spirits, who love nothing better than to lure mortals to destruction. And this is how they set about it:

They take the form of a beautiful chestnut horse, and come out of the water, all saddled and bridled, as if ready to be mounted; then they graze quietly by the side of the road, until some luckless creature is tempted to get on their back.

27

Then they plunge with him into the water, and he is no more seen. (At least, so the old folk say, for I have never met one of these creatures myself.)

To go on with the story, however. The Laird of Morphie knew that the water kelpie who haunted the loch on his property was in the habit of coming out of the water in the gloaming in the way I have described, and grazing quietly by the roadside.

And as he knew also that these uncanny horses were very strong, he determined to gain the mastery over this one, and force it to do his work. And the only way to do this was to take off the magic bridle which it wore and put it on again – no very easy task.

The Laird of Morphie, however, was a man who did not know what fear meant, and he was quite certain that he would be able to conquer the kelpie.

So one evening he took down his sword from the wall, and, calling to his wife, told her that he was in need of a servant, and that he thought the water horse would make a very good one, so he was going out to master him.

'Only,' he added, 'I cannot do it without your help, so listen to what I tell you. You must go out into the garden, and pluck two twigs from the rowan tree that grows by the gate, and fashion them into a Cross, and put it up over the outside of the door, which you must bar and bolt.

'That will keep the creature from entering the house; for no evil spirit can endure the rowan wood, let alone the Holy Sign.

'Then you must open the kitchen window; for although I want to keep the kelpie out, I myself need to get in. Do you understand?'

But if the Laird was not afraid of water horses, his wife was, and, instead of answering him, she threw her arms around his neck and wept bitterly, and begged and besought him not to meddle with spirits, but to bide quietly at home.

Which, of course, he would not agree to do, and he pushed the poor woman away from him roughly, and told her not to be a fool, but to attend to his words and do his bidding. Then he went out and left her, and she was so terrified that she went at once and picked the rowan twigs and made a Cross of them, and put it up outside the door. Then she shut herself into the house, and opened the kitchen window, exactly as her husband had told her to do. After which she crept away to her bed, and hid her head below the blankets.

Meanwhile, the Laird walked boldly down the road, until he came to a place where it ran between two hills, and was out of sight of any house; and in this lonely spot he saw, as he had expected, a fine chestnut horse, nibbling the sweet short grass by the roadside.

It carried a saddle and bridle of the finest leather, and it looked so quiet and docile that it might have been a lady's palfrey.

The Laird was not misled by its looks, however. As he approached it he drew his sword, and when he came up to it he suddenly struck it a sharp rap on the side of the head, completely severing the strap which held its bridle in position.

The creature, taken by surprise, reared high in the air, and, seeing that there was no chance of tempting this cautious mortal to climb on its back, was turning to gallop down to the loch, when its bridle fell from its neck to the ground.

In a moment the Laird had picked it up, and put it into his pocket; for he knew that when a water horse lost its bridle its power was gone, and that it could not go back to its watery abode until it found it again.

No sooner had he done so, than, to his astonishment, the creature began to talk like any mortal, and to beg him to give it back its bridle, reminding him that it had never in its life done him any harm.

'I cannot thank you for that,' said the Laird drily, 'for, methinks, had I once been fool enough to mount on your back we would soon have seen whether you would have done me harm or no. Ha, ha, my bonnie nag, I have your bridle safe in my pocket, and I think I had better keep it there.'

Then the water horse grew angry, and showed his teeth in a way that would have frightened most men.

'You will never set foot in your own house,' he said, 'till you have given me back my bridle; for I can travel quicker than you can, and I will go and take possession of it.'

With these words he galloped off in the direction of the Laird's house.

But the Laird only laughed, and followed at his leisure, for he knew that no spirit, be it witch, or warlock, or demon, could enter a dwelling that was guarded by a Cross of rowan.

And he was right, for when he reached home he found the water horse standing stock still in front of the door, apparently determined that, since it could get no further, it would at least prevent the owner of the house entering.

But, as we know, the kitchen window was open, and the Laird went round the back of the house and jumped in at that.

Then he went upstairs, and put his head out of one of the upper windows, and began to bargain with the kelpie.

'See here,' he said. 'You're very anxious to get your bridle back, for without it you are helpless, and must remain for the remainder of your life on land. I, on my side, have a castle to build, and I need a good strong horse to cart the stones. So if you'll promise to do that for me, I will promise, when you are finished, to give you back your bridle.'

And as there seemed no other way, the water horse agreed to the bargain.

Now, if the kelpie were naturally cruel, I am afraid the

Laird was cruel also, for he loaded the poor beast with such heavy loads that its shoulders were often chafed and bleeding, and it grew thin and miserable-looking.

Indeed, he worked it so hard that it was almost dead by the time the castle was completed.

Then, as he had no further use for it, he gave it back its bridle, and told it that it could go back to where it had come from.

Alas! he did not know what he had laid up in store for himself and his family. For the water kelpie, enraged at the sufferings which it had been made to endure, looked over its shoulder as it was about to plunge into the loch, and solemnly uttered these words:

> *'Sair back, and sair banes,*
> *Drivin' the Laird o' Morphie's stanes!*
> *The Laird o' Morphie'll never thrive*
> *As lang as Kelpie is alive.'*

And his words came only too true; for one misfortune after another fell on the Laird and his descendants, until at last his name died out altogether.

So by this token let all those who read this story learn that it is never wise to persecute anybody, not even a water kelpie.

THE LAIRD O' CO

Elizabeth Grierson

It was a fine summer morning, and the Laird o' Co was having a dander on the green turf outside his castle walls. His real name was the Laird o' Colzean, and his descendants today bear the proud title of Marquises of Ailsa, but all up and down Ayrshire nobody called him anything else than the Laird o' Co; because of the Co's, or sea caves, which were to be found in the rock on which his castle was built.

He was a kind man, and courteous, always ready to be interested in the affairs of his poorer neighbours, and willing to listen to any tale of woe.

So when a little boy came across the green, carrying a small can in his hand, and, pulling his forelock, asked him if he might go to the castle and get a little ale for his sick mother, the Laird gave his consent at once, and, patting the lad on the head, told him to go to the kitchen and ask for the butler, and tell him that he, the Laird, had given orders that his can was to be filled with the best ale that was in the cellar.

Away the boy went, and found the old butler, who, after

listening to his message, took him down into the cellar, and proceeded to carry out his master's orders.

There was one cask of particularly fine ale, which was kept entirely for the Laird's own use, which had been opened some time before, and which was now about half full.

'I will fill the bairn's can out o' this,' thought the old man to himself. ''Tis both nourishing and light – the very thing for sick folk.' So, taking the can from the child's hand, he proceeded to draw the ale.

But what was his astonishment to find that, although the ale flowed freely enough from the barrel, the little can, which could not have held more than a quarter of a gallon, remained always just half full.

The ale poured into it in a clear amber stream, until the big cask was quite empty, and still the quantity that was in the little can did not seem to increase.

The butler could not understand it. He looked at the

cask, and then he looked at the can; then he looked down at the floor at his feet to see if he had not spilt any.

No, the ale had not disappeared in that way, for the cellar floor was as white, and dry, and clean, as possible.

Plague on the can; it must be bewitched, thought the old man, and his short, stubby hair stood up like porcupine quills round his bald head, for if there was anything on earth of which he had a mortal dread, it was warlocks, and witches, and suchlike bogles.

'I'm not going to open up another barrel,' he said, gruffly, handing back the half-filled can to the lad. 'So ye may just go home with what is there; the Laird's ale is too good to waste on a whipper-snapper like you.'

But the boy stood his ground. A promise was a promise, and the Laird had both promised, and sent orders to the butler that the can was to be filled, so the boy would not go home till it was filled.

It was in vain that the old man first argued, and then grew angry – the boy would not stir a step.

'The Laird had said that he was to get the ale, and the ale he must have.'

At last the perturbed butler left him standing there, and hurried off to his master to tell him he was convinced that the can was bewitched, for it had swallowed up a whole half cask of ale, and after doing so it was only half full; and to ask if he would come down himself, and order the lad off the premises.

'Not I,' said the genial Laird, 'for the lad is quite right. I promised that he should have his can full of ale to take home to his sick mother, and he shall have it if it takes all the barrels in my cellar to fill it. So go back to the cellar again, and open up another cask.'

The butler dare not disobey; so he reluctantly retraced his steps, but, as he went, he shook his head sadly, for it seemed to him that not only the boy with the can, but his master also, was bewitched.

When he reached the cellar he found the bairn waiting patiently where he had left him, and, without wasting further words, he took the can from his hand and broached another barrel.

If he had been astonished before, he was more astonished now. Scarce had a couple of drops fallen from the tap, than the boy's can was full to the brim.

'Take it, laddie, and begone, with all speed,' he said, glad to get the can out of his fingers; and the boy did not wait for a second bidding. Thanking the butler most earnestly for his trouble, and paying no attention to the fact that the old man had not been so civil to him as he might have been, he departed. Nor, though the butler took pains to ask all round the countryside, was anything heard of him again, nor of anyone who knew anything about him, or anything about his sick mother.

Years passed by, and sore trouble fell upon the House o' Co. For the Laird went to fight in the wars in Flanders, and, chancing to be taken prisoner, he was shut up in prison, and condemned to death. Alone, in a foreign country, he had no friends to speak for him, and escape seemed hopeless.

It was the night before his execution, and he was sitting in his lonely cell, thinking sadly of his wife and children, whom he never expected to see again. At the thought of them the picture of his home rose clearly in his mind – the grand old castle standing on its rock above the Firth of Clyde, and the bonnie daisy-spangled stretch of links which lay before its gates, where he had been wont to take a dander in the sweet summer mornings. Then, all unbidden, a vision of the little lad carrying the can, who had come to beg ale for his sick mother, and whom he had long ago forgotten, rose up before him.

The vision was so clear and distinct that he felt almost as if he were acting the scene over again, and he rubbed his eyes to get rid of it, feeling that, if he had to die tomorrow, it was time that he turned his thoughts to higher things.

But as he did so the door of his cell flew noiselessly open, and there, on the threshold, stood the self-same little lad, looking not a day older, with his finger on his lip, and a mysterious smile upon his face.

> *'Laird o' Co,*
> *Rise and go!'*

he whispered, beckoning to him to follow him. Needless to say, the Laird did so, too much amazed to think of asking questions.

Through the long passages of the prison the little lad went, the Laird close at his heels; and whenever he came to a locked door, he had but to touch it, and it opened before them, so that in no long time they were safe outside the walls.

The overjoyed Laird would have overwhelmed his little deliverer with words of thanks had not the boy held up his hand to stop him. 'Get on my back,' he said shortly, 'for you are not safe till you are right out of this country.'

The Laird did as he was bid, and, marvellous as it seems, the boy was quite able to bear his weight. As soon as the Laird was comfortably seated the pair set off, over sea and land, and never stopped till, in almost less time than it takes to tell it, the boy set him down, in the early dawn, on the daisy-spangled green in front of his castle, just where he had spoken first to him so many years before.

Then he turned, and laid his little hand on the Laird's big one:

> *'Ae gude turn deserves anither,*
> *Tak' ye that for being sae kind to my auld mither,'*

he said, and vanished.

And from that day to this he has never been seen again.

THE BROWNIE O'
FERNE-DEN

Elizabeth Grierson

There have been many brownies known in Scotland; and stories have been written about the Brownie o' Bodsbeck and the Brownie o' Blednock, but about neither of them has a prettier story been told than that which I am going to tell you about the Brownie o' Ferne-Den.

Now, Ferne-Den was a farmhouse, which got its name from the glen, or 'den', on the edge of which it stood, and through which anyone who wished to reach the dwelling had to pass.

And this glen was believed to be the abode of a brownie, who never appeared to anyone in the daytime, but who, it was said, was sometimes seen at night, stealing about, like an ungainly shadow, from tree to tree, trying to keep out of sight, and never, by any chance, harming anybody.

Indeed, like all brownies that are properly treated and let alone, so far was he from harming anyone, that he was always on the look-out to do a good turn to those who needed his assistance. The farmer often said that he did not know what he would do without him; for if there was any work to be finished in a hurry at the farm – corn to thresh, or winnow, or tie up into bags, turnips to cut, clothes to wash, corn-sheaves to be kirned, a garden to be weeded – all that the farmer and his wife had to do was to leave the door of the barn, or the turnip shed, or the milk house open when they went to bed, and put down a bowl of new milk on the doorstep for the Brownie's supper, and when they woke the next morning the bowl would be empty, and the job finished better than if it had been done by mortal hands.

In spite of all this, however, which might have proved to them how gentle and kindly the creature really was, everyone about the place was afraid of him, and would rather go a couple of miles round about in the dark, when they were coming home from kirk or market, than pass through the glen, and run the risk of catching a glimpse of him.

I said that they were all afraid of him, but that was not true, for the farmer's wife was so good and gentle that she was not afraid of anything on God's earth, and when the Brownie's supper had to be left outside, she always filled his bowl with the richest milk, and added a good spoonful of cream to it, for, said she, 'He works so hard for us, and asks no wages, he well deserves the very best meal that we can give him.'

One night this gentle lady was taken very ill, and everyone was afraid that she was going to die. Of course, her husband was greatly distressed, and so were her servants, for she had been such a good mistress to them that they loved her as if she had been their mother. But they were all young, and none of them knew very much about illness, and everyone agreed that it would be better to send off for an old woman who lived about seven miles away on the other side of the river, who was known to be a very skilful nurse.

But who was to go? That was the question. For it was black midnight, and the way to the old woman's house lay straight through the glen. And whoever travelled that road ran the risk of meeting the dreaded Brownie.

The farmer would have gone only too willingly, but he dare not leave his wife alone; and the servants stood in groups about the kitchen, each one telling the other that he ought to go, yet no one offering to go themselves.

Little did they think that the cause of all their terror, a queer, wee, misshapen little man, all covered with hair, with a long beard, red-rimmed eyes, broad, flat feet like a frog's, and enormous long arms that touched the ground, even when he stood upright, was within a yard or two of them, listening to their talk, with an anxious face, behind the kitchen door.

For he had come up as usual, from his hiding-place in the glen, to see if there was any work for him to do, and to look for his bowl of milk. And he had seen, from the open door and lit-up windows, that there was something wrong inside the farmhouse, which at that hour was usually dark, and still, and silent; and he had crept into the entry to try and find out what the matter was.

When he gathered from the servants' talk that the mistress, whom he too loved so dearly, and who had been so kind to him, was ill, his heart sank within him; and when he heard that the silly servants were so taken up with their own fears that they dared not set out to fetch a nurse for her, his contempt and anger knew no bounds.

'Fools, idiots, dolts!' he muttered to himself, stamping his queer, misshapen feet on the floor. 'They speak as if a body were ready to take a bite off them as soon as ever he met them. If they only knew the bother it gives me to keep out of their road they wouldna be so silly. But, by my troth, if they go on like this, the bonnie lady will die amongst their fingers. So it strikes me that Brownie must just gang himself.'

So saying, he reached up his hand, and took down a dark

cloak which belonged to the farmer, and was hanging on a peg on the wall. Throwing it over his head and shoulders in an effort to hide his ungainly form, he hurried away to the stable, and saddled and bridled the fleetest-footed horse that stood there.

When the last buckle was fastened, he led the horse to the door, and scrambled on its back. 'Now, if you ever travelled fast, travel fast now,' he said; and it was as if the creature understood him, for it gave a little whinny and pricked up its ears; then it darted out into the darkness like an arrow from the bow.

In less time than the distance had ever been ridden in before, the Brownie drew rein at the old woman's cottage.

She was in bed, fast asleep; but he rapped sharply on the window, and when she rose and put her old face, framed in its white mutch, close to the pane to ask who was there, he bent forward and told her his errand.

'You must come with me, Goodwife, and that quickly,' he

commanded, in his deep, harsh voice, 'if the lady of Ferne-Den's life is to be saved; for there is no one to nurse her up-bye at the farm there, save a lot of empty-headed servant wenches.'

'But how am I to get there? Have they sent a cart for me?' asked the old woman anxiously; for, as far as she could see, there was nothing at the door save a horse and its rider.

'No, they have sent no cart,' replied the Brownie, shortly. 'So you must just climb up behind me on the saddle, and hang on tight to my waist, and I'll promise to land ye at Ferne-Den safe and sound.'

His voice was so masterful that the old woman dare not refuse to do as she was bid; besides, she had often ridden pillion-wise when she was a lassie, so she made haste to dress herself, and when she was ready she unlocked her door, and, mounting the louping-on stane that stood beside it, she was soon seated behind the dark-cloaked stranger, with her arms clasped tightly round him.

Not a word was spoken till they approached the dreaded glen, then the old woman felt her courage giving way. 'Do ye think that there will be any chance of meeting the Brownie?' she asked timidly. 'I would fain not run the risk, for folk say that he is an ill-omened creature.'

Her companion gave a curious laugh. 'Keep up your heart, and dinna talk havers,' he said, 'for I promise ye ye'll see naught uglier this night than the man whom ye ride behind.'

'Oh, then, I'm fine and safe,' replied the old woman, with a sigh of relief; 'for although I havena' seen your face, I warrant that ye are a true man, for the care you have taken of a poor old woman.'

She relapsed into silence again till the glen was passed and the good horse had turned into the farmyard. Then the horseman slid to the ground, and, turning round, lifted her carefully down in his long, strong arms. As he did so the cloak slipped off him, revealing his short, broad body and his misshapen limbs.

'In a' the world, what kind o' man are ye?' she asked, peering into his face in the grey morning light, which was just dawning. 'What makes your eyes so big? And what have ye done to your feet? They are more like frog's webs than anything else.'

The queer little man laughed again. 'I've wandered many a mile in my time without a horse to help me, and I've heard it said that ower-much walking makes the feet unshapely,' he replied. 'But waste no time in talking, good Dame. Go your way into the house; and, hark'ee, if anyone asks you who brought you hither so quickly, tell them that there was a lack of men, so you just had to be content to ride behind the Brownie o' Ferne-Den.'

KATHERINE CRACKERNUTS

Elizabeth Grierson

There was once a King whose wife died, leaving him with an only daughter, whom he dearly loved. The little Princess's name was Velvet-Cheek, and she was so good, and bonnie, and kind-hearted that all her father's subjects loved her. But as the King was generally engaged in transacting the business of the State, the poor little maiden had rather a lonely life, and often wished that she had a sister with whom she could play, and who would be a companion to her.

The King, hearing this, made up his mind to marry a middle-aged countess, whom he had met at a neighbouring court, who had one daughter, named Katherine, who was just a little younger than the Princess Velvet-Cheek, and who, he thought, would make a nice playfellow for her.

He did so, and in one way the arrangement turned out very well, for the two girls loved one another dearly, and had everything in common, just as if they had really been sisters.

But in another way it turned out very badly, for the new Queen was a cruel and ambitious woman, and she wanted her own daughter to do as she had done, and make a grand marriage, and perhaps even become a queen. And when she saw that Princess Velvet-Cheek was growing into a very beautiful young woman – more beautiful by far than her own daughter – she began to hate her, and to wish that in some way she would lose her good looks.

'For,' thought she, 'what suitor will heed my daughter as long as her stepsister is by her side?'

Now, among the servants and retainers at her husband's castle there was an old henwife, who, men said, was in league with the evil spirits of the air, and who was skilled in the knowledge of charms, and philtres, and love potions.

'Perhaps she could help me to do what I seek to do,' said the wicked Queen; and one night, when it was growing dusk, she wrapped a cloak round her, and set out to this old henwife's cottage.

'Send the lassie to me tomorrow morning before she has broken her fast,' replied the old dame when she heard what her visitor had to say. 'I will find out a way to mar her beauty.' And the wicked Queen went home content.

Next morning she went to the Princess's room while she was dressing, and told her to go out before breakfast and get the eggs that the henwife had gathered. 'And see,' added she, 'that you don't eat anything before you go, for there is nothing that makes the roses bloom on a young maiden's cheeks like going out fasting in the fresh morning air.'

Princess Velvet-Cheek promised to do as she was bid, and go and fetch the eggs; but as she was not fond of going out of doors before she had had something to eat, and as, moreover, she suspected that her stepmother had some hidden reason for giving her such an unusual order, and she did not trust her stepmother's hidden reasons, she slipped into the pantry as she went downstairs and helped herself to a large slice of cake. Then, after she had eaten it, she went straight to the henwife's cottage and asked for the eggs.

'Lift the lid of that pot there, your Highness, and you will see them,' said the old woman, pointing to the big pot standing in the corner in which she boiled her hens' meat.

The Princess did so, and found a heap of eggs lying inside, which she lifted into her basket, while the old woman watched her with a curious smile.

'Go home to your lady mother, hinny,' she said at last, 'and tell her from me to keep the press door better snibbit.'

The Princess went home, and gave this extraordinary message to her stepmother, wondering to herself meanwhile what it meant.

But if she did not understand the henwife's words, the Queen understood them only too well. For from them she gathered that the Princess had in some way prevented the old witch's spell doing what she intended it to do.

So next morning, when she sent her stepdaughter once more on the same errand, she accompanied her to the door of the castle herself, so that the poor girl had no chance of paying a visit to the pantry. But as she went along the road that led to the cottage, she felt so hungry that, when she passed a party of country-folk picking peas by the roadside, she asked them to give her a handful.

They did so, and she ate the peas; and so it came about that the same thing happened that had happened yesterday.

The henwife sent her to look for the eggs; but she could work no spell upon her, because she had broken her fast. So the old woman bade her go home again and give the same message to the Queen.

The Queen was very angry when she heard it, for she felt that she was being outwitted by this slip of a girl, and she determined that, although she was not fond of getting up early, she would accompany her next day herself, and make sure that she had nothing to eat as she went.

So next morning she walked with the Princess to the henwife's cottage, and, as had happened twice before, the old woman sent the royal maiden to lift the lid off the pot in the corner in order to get the eggs.

And the moment that the Princess did so off jumped her own pretty head, and on jumped that of a sheep.

Then the wicked Queen thanked the cruel old witch for the service that she had rendered to her, and went home quite delighted with the success of her scheme; while the poor Princess picked up her own head and put it into her basket along with the eggs, and went home crying, keeping behind the hedge all the way, for she felt so ashamed of her sheep's head that she was afraid that anyone saw her.

Now, as I told you, the Princess's stepsister Katherine loved her dearly, and when she saw what a cruel deed had been wrought on her she was so angry that she declared that she would not remain another hour in the castle. 'For,' said she, 'if my mother can order one such deed to be done, who can hinder her ordering another? I think it's better for us both to be where she cannot reach us.'

So she wrapped a fine silk shawl round her poor step-sister's head, so that none could tell what it was like, and, putting the real head in the basket, she took her by the hand, and the two set out to seek their fortunes.

They walked and they walked, till they reached a splendid palace, and when they came to it Katherine made as though she would go boldly up and knock at the door.

'I may perchance find work here,' she explained, 'and earn enough money to keep us both in comfort.'

But the poor Princess would fain have pulled her back. 'They will have nothing to do with you,' she whispered, 'when they see that you have a sister with a sheep's head.'

'And who is to know that you have a sheep's head?' asked Katherine. 'Just hold your tongue, and keep the shawl well round your face, and leave the rest to me.'

So up she went and knocked at the kitchen door, and when the housekeeper came to answer it she asked her if there was any work that she could give her to do. 'For,' said she, 'I have a sick sister, who is sore troubled with the migraine in her head, and I would fain find a quiet lodging for her where she could rest for the night.'

'Do you know how to nurse a sickness?' asked the housekeeper, who was greatly struck by Katherine's soft voice and gentle ways.

'Ay, I do,' replied Katherine, 'for when one's sister is troubled with the migraine, one has to learn to look after her, and to go about softly and not to make a noise.'

Now it chanced that the King's eldest son, the Crown Prince, was lying ill in the palace with a strange disease, which seemed to have touched his brain. For he was so restless, especially at nights, that someone had always to be with him to watch that he did himself no harm; and this state of things had gone on so long that everyone was quite worn out.

And the old housekeeper thought that it would be a good chance to get a quiet night's sleep if this capable-looking stranger could be trusted to sit up with the Prince.

So she left her at the door, and went and consulted the King; and the King came out and spoke to Katherine, and he, too, was so pleased with her voice and her appearance that he gave orders that a room should be set apart in the castle for her sick sister and herself, and he promised that, if she would sit up that night with the Prince, and see that he came to no harm, she would have, as her reward, a bag of silver pennies in the morning.

Katherine agreed to the bargain readily, *For*, thought she, *'twill always be a night's lodging for the Princess; and, forbye that, a bag of silver pennies is not to be got every day*.

So the Princess went to bed in the comfortable chamber that was set apart for her, and Katherine went to watch by the sick Prince.

He was a handsome, comely young man, who seemed to be in some sort of fever, for his brain was not quite clear, and he tossed and tumbled from side to side, gazing anxiously in front of him, and stretching out his hands as if he were in search of something.

And at twelve o'clock at night, just when Katherine thought that he was going to fall into a refreshing sleep, what was her horror to see him rise from his bed, dress himself hastily, open the door, and slip downstairs, as if he were going to look for somebody.

'There's something strange in this,' said the girl to herself. 'I'd better follow him and see what happens.'

So she stole out of the room after the Prince and followed him safely downstairs; and what was her astonishment to find that apparently he was going some distance, for he put on his hat and riding-coat, and, unlocking the door, crossed the courtyard to the stable, and began to saddle his horse.

When he had done so, he led it out, and mounted, and, whistling softly to a hound which lay asleep in a corner, he prepared to ride away.

'I must go too, and see the end of this,' said Katherine bravely; 'I'm sure he's bewitched. These are not the actions of a sick man.'

So, just as the horse was about to start, she jumped lightly on its back, and settled herself comfortably behind its rider, all unnoticed by him.

Then this strange pair rode away through the woods, and, as they went, Katherine pulled the hazel-nuts that nodded in great clusters in her face. 'For,' said she to herself, 'dear only knows where next I may get anything to eat.'

On and on they rode, till they left the greenwood far behind them and came out on an open moor. Soon they reached a hillock, and here the Prince drew rein, and, stooping down, cried in a strange, uncanny whisper, 'Open,

open, green hill, and let the Prince, and his horse, and his hound enter.'

'And,' whispered Katherine quickly, 'let his lady enter behind him.'

Instantly, to her great astonishment, the top of the knowe seemed to tip up, leaving an aperture large enough for the little company to enter; then it closed gently behind them again.

They found themselves in a magnificent hall, brilliantly lighted by hundreds of candles stuck in sconces round the walls. In the centre of this apartment was a group of the most beautiful maidens that Katherine had ever seen, all dressed in shimmering ball-gowns, with wreaths of roses and violets in their hair. And there were sprightly youths also, who had been treading a measure with these beauteous damsels to the strains of fairy music.

When the maidens saw the Prince, they ran to him, and led him away to join their revels. And at the touch of their hands all his languor seemed to disappear, and he became the brightest of all the throng, and laughed, and danced, and sang as if he had never known what it was to be ill.

As no one took any notice of Katherine, she sat down quietly on a bit of rock to watch what would befall. And as she watched, she became aware of a little wee bairnie, playing with a tiny wand, quite close to her feet.

He was a bonnie bit bairn, and she was just thinking of trying to make friends with him when one of the beautiful maidens passed, and, looking at the wand, said to her partner, in a meaning tone, 'Three strokes of that wand would give Katherine's sister back her pretty face.'

Here was news indeed! Katherine's breath came thick and fast; and with trembling fingers she drew some of the nuts out of her pocket, and began rolling them carelessly towards the child. Apparently he did not get nuts very often, for he dropped his little wand at once, and stretched out his tiny hands to pick them up.

This was just what she wanted; and she slipped down from her seat to the ground, and drew a little nearer to him. Then she threw one or two more nuts in his way, and, when he was picking these up, she managed to lift the wand unobserved, and to hide it under her apron. After this, she crept cautiously back to her seat again; and not a moment too soon, for just then a cock crew, and at the sound the whole troop of dancers vanished – all but the Prince, who ran to mount his horse, and was in such a hurry to be gone that Katherine had much ado to get up behind him before the hillock opened, and he rode swiftly into the outer world once more.

But she managed it, and, as they rode homewards in the grey morning light, she sat and cracked her nuts and ate them as fast as she could, for her adventures had made her marvellously hungry.

When she and her strange patient had once more reached the castle, she just waited to see him go back to bed, and

50

begin to toss and tumble as he had done before; then she ran to her stepsister's room, and, finding her asleep, with her poor misshapen head lying peacefully on the pillow, she gave it three sharp little strokes with the fairy wand, and, lo and behold! the sheep's head vanished, and the Princess's own pretty one took its place.

In the morning the King and the old housekeeper came to enquire what kind of night the Prince had had. Katherine answered that he had had a very good night; for she was very anxious to stay with him longer, and now that she had found out that the elfin maidens who dwelt in the green knowe had thrown a spell over him, she was resolved to find out also how that spell could be broken.

And fortune favoured her; for the King was so pleased to think that such a suitable nurse had been found for the Prince, and he was also so charmed with the looks of her stepsister, who came out of her chamber as bright and bonnie as in the old days, declaring that her migraine was all gone, and that she was now able to do any work that the housekeeper might find for her, that he begged Katherine to stay with his son a little longer, adding that, if she would do so, he would give her a bag of gold sovereigns.

So Katherine agreed readily; and that night she watched by the Prince as she had done the night before. And at twelve o'clock he rose and dressed himself, and rode to the fairy knowe, just as she had expected him to do, for she was now quite certain that the poor young man was bewitched, and not suffering from a fever, as everyone thought he was.

And you may be sure that she accompanied him, riding behind him all unnoticed, and filling her pockets with nuts as she rode.

When they reached the fairy knowe, he spoke the same words that he had spoken the night before. 'Open, open, green hill, and let the young Prince, and his horse, and his hound enter.' And when the green hill opened, Katherine added softly, 'And his lady behind him.' So they all passed in together.

Once again, Katherine seated herself on a stone, and looked around her. The same revels were going on as yesternight, and the Prince was soon in the thick of them, dancing and laughing madly. The girl watched him narrowly, wondering if she would ever be able to find out what would restore him to his right mind; and, as she was watching him, the same little bairn who had played with the magic wand came up to her again. Only this time he was playing with a little bird.

And as he played, one of the dancers passed by, and, turning to her partner, said lightly, 'Three bites of that birdie would lift the Prince's sickness, and make him as well as he ever was.' Then she joined in the dance again, leaving Katherine sitting upright on her stone quivering with excitement.

If only she could get that bird the Prince might be cured! Very carefully she began to shake some nuts out of her pocket, and roll them across the floor towards the child.

He picked them up eagerly, letting go the bird as he did so; and, in an instant, Katherine caught it, and hid it under her apron.

In no long time after that the cock crew, and the Prince and she set out on their homeward ride. But this morning, instead of cracking nuts, she killed and plucked the bird; then she put it on a spit in front of the fire and began to roast it.

And soon it began to frizzle, and get brown, and smell deliciously, and the Prince, in his bed in the corner, opened his eyes and murmured faintly, 'How I wish I had a bite of that birdie.'

When she heard the words Katherine's heart jumped for joy, and as soon as the bird was roasted she cut a little piece from its breast and popped it into the Prince's mouth.

When he had eaten it his strength seemed to come back somewhat, for he rose on his elbow and looked at his nurse. 'Oh! if I had but another bite of that birdie!' he said. And his voice was certainly stronger.

So Katherine gave him another piece, and when he had eaten that he sat right up in bed.

'Oh! if I had but a third bite o' that birdie!' he cried. And now the colour was coming right back into his face, and his eyes were shining.

This time Katherine brought him the whole of the rest of the bird; and he ate it up greedily, picking the bones quite clean with his fingers; and when it was finished, he sprang out of bed and dressed himself, and sat down by the fire.

And when the King came in the morning, with his old housekeeper at his back, to see how the Prince was, he found him sitting cracking nuts with his nurse, for Katherine had brought home quite a lot in her apron pocket.

The King was so delighted to find his son cured that he gave all the credit to Katherine Crackernuts, as he called her, and he gave orders at once that the Prince should marry her. 'For,' said he, 'a maiden who is such a good nurse is sure to make a good queen.'

The Prince was quite willing to do as his father bade him; and, while they were talking together, his younger brother came in, leading Princess Velvet-Cheek by the hand, whose acquaintance he had made but yesterday, declaring that he had fallen in love with her, and that he wanted to marry her immediately.

So it all turned out very well, and everybody was quite pleased; and the two weddings took place at once, and, unless they be dead since that time, the young couples are living yet.

TAM LIN

Traditional

Carterhaugh is a lonely part of Ettrickdale in the Scottish Borders. People used to say it was a haunted, elvan country, with a fairy well in the pinewoods. This was the rhyme they used to say to their daughters:

> *'Oh I forbid you, maidens a',*
> *That wear gowd on your hair,*
> *To come or gae by Carterhaugh,*
> *For young Tam Lin is there.'*

The name of Tam Lin was famous throughout the Borders. He was a young man whom the fairies had stolen away from humankind. Any girl who entered the Carterhaugh pinewoods and found the fairy well would come under Tam's spell and pay Tam's price.

The Laird of Carterhaugh had a young daughter called Janet – a high-spirited, bonny lass with golden hair. One spring day, Janet decided she would ignore the warnings

about the pinewood. Slipping away from her father's Hall, she entered the wood to see if she could find the fairy well. She was wearing her green kirtle, and a gold band in her golden hair. When at last she found a well, deep in the forest, she found a tethered white horse grazing quietly beside it. But there was no sign of the notorious Tam Lin. Sitting down at the side of the well under a rosebush, Janet plucked a double white rose to pin on her gown. No sooner had she done this than a young man appeared, as if from nowhere. He was tall and handsome, and he had deep grey eyes and dark silken hair. It was Tam Lin.

'What brings ye to my wood, lady, and why are ye picking roses from my well?' he asked.

'Carterhaugh is my father's estate,' said Janet, a bold smile playing in her eyes. 'So I'll come and go in Carterhaugh and ask no leave of you or any man.'

'Will you indeed, brave lass,' said Tam with a silken laugh. 'This wood belongs to the fairy folk and I am here to protect it for them.'

'Are you one of them?' Janet whispered, bold no longer. All of a sudden there seemed something strange about the young man standing at her side in the fading light.

'I am indeed,' Tam smiled, bowing low to her. 'But I was not always one of them. Come with me, Janet, and I will show ye all the flowers of the forest.'

And so they explored the forest of Carterhaugh, which Janet had never before visited, in the half-light of the gloaming.

'I must go,' Janet said at last. 'They will be looking for me. I have been gone a long time.'

'Not so very long,' laughed handsome Tam. 'Not so very long.'

And indeed, when Janet returned to the Hall from the enchanted wood, no one had even noticed she had been away.

Of course, Janet was in love with the mysterious and handsome Tam Lin. Who was he? How had she never seen him before? Was he not a real mortal man? All summer long, she could think of nothing and no one else. And so, at last, she plucked up courage to return to the wood to see her lover. It was autumn now as she made her way back through the pinewood to the well. Once again the white horse was tethered by the well, but there was no sign of Tam. However, there were still roses on the rosebush, and Janet plucked a flower. And once again, Tam appeared from nowhere, as if he had been waiting for her.

'Tell me, Tam Lin,' said Janet, looking into his deep grey eyes. 'I must know this – tell me who you are. Are you a Christian man, or are you one of the fairy folk?'

Tam looked at her for a long time. At last, he shook his head and said, 'Aye, I'll tell ye the hale sorry story. My grandfaither was the Earl of Roxburgh. One cold, snell day we were riding back frae the hunting, and I fell frae my horse on yon green mound. The Queen o' Fairies caught me there and I've lived with her ever since. She's a pleasant enough mistress in some ways, but I am in thrall to her, and must obey her commands. And she's no exactly a *guid* fairy. Every seven years she pays a human tithe to hell, and I'm feared the next time'll be my turn.

'If ye love me, Janet, ye can save me,' Tam continued, and now there was a plea in his tone. 'This nicht is Hallowe'en and tomorrow is All-Hallows day. So this is the one nicht in the year ye can save me. Hark carefully to what I tell ye.

'Just at the mirk and midnight hour – no sooner and no later – the fairy folk will ride in procession through the wood. I will be with them. If ye would win your ain true love, ye will come here this nicht.'

'But how shall I ken ye, Tam Lin,' asked Janet, 'among so many folk, and in a dark midnight wood?'

'Here is what ye must do,' said Tam. 'I will be mounted on the third horse. Let pass the black and the brown horses, but quickly run to the third horse – this milk-white steed ye see before ye – and pull ye his rider down. I will be that rider – my right hand gloved, my left hand bare, my bonnet well back, uncovered my hair.

'Hold me tight and fast in your arms for dear life, lady. They'll turn me into all sorts of beasts and crawlies – a newt, then an adder, then a bear, a lion, and a red-hot iron bar – and last of all, a burning lead weight. Then – and only then – ye may throw me with all speed into the water of the well. If ye do all this, then I will be your true love for ever, and I'll climb out of the well a mortal man once more. Wrap me then in your green mantle, Janet, and I shall be saved from the Fairy Queen. And remember that if ye love me, nothing can hurt ye.'

Janet listened as Tam spoke, and promised with a shiver to do as he had bidden. The next night – a very dark, moonless Hallowe'en – she put on her warm green mantle, crept from the house and ran silently to the now black, enchanted wood.

Exactly at the midnight hour, she heard the ring of bells on bridles as the fairy folk came riding down the glade. There was a shimmer of dim light from the fairy lanterns, just enough to see the Queen on her black stallion leading her troop through the trees. Then came a second horse, glowing silver-green among the trees. The third horse was a milk-white steed, just as Tam had promised. Janet jumped forward and dragged its rider from the milk-white horse, and hung on to him for dear life.

Then the fairies were screeching and screaming around her. There was a green flash, and Janet suddenly felt herself holding a loathly, slimy newt. Or was it a snake, winding and coiling itself about her arms and throat? Janet's instinct was to hurl the writhing thing from her, but she remembered Tam's plea and his plight and his promise, and she held firm. Then the snake turned itself into a growling, hairy bear, and then a lion whose hot, foul breath knocked her to the forest floor. Still Janet held fast to her burden. Then there was the shrieking pain of a red-hot iron, and she would fain have flung it from her. But she held on. And then there was the deadly weight of burning hot lead. Struggling to the edge of the well, Janet at last managed to tip her agonizing burden into the dark waters of the well. There was an almighty splash and then a great hiss of steam – and Tam Lin clambered from the water, wet and shaken but even more handsome than before.

Out then spake the Queen o' Fairies, out of a bush of broom. 'Curse you, madam. You have stolen my bonniest knight, my stately groom,' she shrieked, and an angry queen was she.

But the happy pair were now beyond the magic powers of the Fairy Queen. Janet's love was stronger than the Queen's magic, and the Queen knew she was beaten. Janet and Tam fled back to the Hall, swiftly and safely, where they were welcomed with great joy. They lived together in great happiness all their lives, and in the fullness of time their bonny son became the Laird of Carterhaugh.

THOMAS RYMER

Traditional

Long ago, the town of Earlston in Lauderdale in the Scottish Borders was just a tiny hamlet, called Ercildoune. In those days, Thomas Rymer was a well-known local character, for he was the Laird of Ercildoune. He was a gifted harpist, and he was always making up songs and rhymes. People often saw him sitting by the roadside playing his little harp and trying out a new song. Or they'd see him driving his cattle to the village market, his little harp slung across his shoulder.

As a young man, Thomas was a great one for the lassies of Lauderdale. He was aye teasing them, joking with them, singing their praises on his harp, and flirting with them. He often left his cattle to wander off while he was chatting up a local lovely.

One May morning, he was sitting by the Huntlie Burn playing on his harp. His back to a great thorn tree called the Eildon Tree, he was picking out a magic, haunted melody when all at once he spied a lady ride down by the waterside.

She was all clad in shimmering green – the colour of the fairy folk – and she rode on a milk-white steed. The bells of her horse's bridle jingled merrily as she rode along.

Thomas thought he had never seen such a gorgeous vision, and he couldn't take his eyes off the lovely lady. His song faltered and finally petered out, and he rose unsteadily to his feet. Saluting the lady with a low bow, he whispered to her, 'Greetings, Madam. You must be the Queen of Heaven.'

'Oh no, no, Thomas,' she replied. 'That is not my name. But I am the Queen of fair Elfland, and I've come to visit you. I heard your singing – please play on. I would fain listen to you all day. When you've finished your song, you may kiss my lips. And then you will have to come with me to Elfland.'

'That's not a prospect to frighten me,' said Thomas quickly.

'But,' said the Queen, 'one kiss of my rosy, red lips will seal a stiff fate upon you: you will have to serve me in Elfland for seven years – through weal or woe, good times or bad.'

The Queen's sweet charms already had Thomas completely under her spell, and when his song was done he kissed her long and hard. Then she jumped up on her milk-white steed, and Thomas jumped up behind her. And with bridle jingling merrily, the pair of them sped off swifter than the wind, over fields and moors and mountains.

At last, they came to a fork where three roads met. The Queen showed Thomas first a narrow track into the hills beset with thorns and briars: this was the path of righteousness, taken by few travellers on life's journey. The second road was broad and flat and grassy: it led through a pretty meadow, and was the busy path to wickedness. Thomas had heard about these paths from the priest at the little church of Ercildoune. But the Queen and Thomas took the third road, the winding fernie brae leading to fair Elfland, and they duly reached their destination in the deep woods as the shadows lengthened and mirk night was falling.

'One other thing, Thomas,' said the Queen when they arrived at her country. 'You will be with me for seven years. And during all that time you must hold your tongue and not speak. *Not one word!* If you speak so much as one word, you will be my servant for ever. And you will not see Ercildoune again.'

When Thomas came to the Other Country, he was well looked after. He was given a silken green outfit, just like the other fairy folk, and he served the Queen loyally and happily for seven years. For her pleasure he would often play his harp, and her court would often dance to his sweet music. And in all the time of his service at the court of the Queen of Elfland, he uttered not a single word of human speech.

> *And till seven years were gane and past*
> *True Thomas on Earth was never seen.*

Then one day the Queen spoke to Thomas. 'Our seven years are gone, Thomas, and you must return home. You have served me well. And you have kept your silence. I shall miss you.'

So Thomas Rymer was free once again, and he made his way back to Ercildoune. When they parted, the Queen gave him a large apple from her orchard. 'Eat this,' she said. 'It will give you two precious gifts – of truth and of prophecy. And it will make you rich and famous. Farewell, Thomas.'

Thomas wasn't at all sure if he *wanted* these fairy gifts. 'I've always had a guid Scots tongue in my head,' he thought to himself. 'But I've also known when to hold it! Truth is a two-edged weapon, it seems to me. But we'll see . . .' He wasn't too sure about the gift of prophecy either: did he *really* want to be able to see into the future?

So Thomas returned quietly to Ercildoune to his wife and children. His wife's black hair was flecked with grey now, and his children were all young men and women. Thomas was quite a changed person too – older and quieter, and flirting no more. He had eaten the apple, and now it was as if he noticed all the blemishes of the lassies of Lauderdale. And because now he always spoke the truth, the lassies didn't like him nearly so much. It was one thing to tell a girl that her hair was golden – but quite another to tell her it looked like a haystack!

But Thomas still played his harp and made up songs, even if there was now often a far-away look in his eyes. Everyone wanted to know where he'd been, of course. But strangely enough no one ever dared quiz him about his absence, so it was never talked about.

Thomas Rymer began to get a name as a wise man in Ercildoune – a person who always spoke the truth, and who could really prophesy the future. He became known as True Thomas, and his fame as a seer spread rapidly throughout Scotland after he foretold the death of King Alexander III one stormy March night in the year 1286. When Alexander was indeed killed in a fall from his horse on the cliffs near Kinghorn in Fife, exactly as Thomas had described, people started to come from far and near to consult Thomas about all sorts of matters. Farmers were forever wanting his advice about the weather, pilgrims often wanted to know if it would be wise for them to postpone a pilgrimage to Whithorn or St Andrews, indeed there was soon a constant stream of visitors to Thomas's door, and all paying him handsomely for his prophecies.

And so Thomas became rich and famous, just as the Fairy Queen had said he would. But sometimes his visitors had great difficulty getting through to him – because his mind had taken him back to fair Elfland and his Fairy Queen.

One evening, when Thomas was sitting in a vacant trance

beside his moonlit door, one of his sons came to whisper in his ear. 'They say there is a white doe grazing at the entrance to the park.' Now Thomas knew that a white deer is almost certainly a visitor from the Other Country. Without a word to anyone, he took his harp from its hook and slung it over his shoulder. Then he slipped out into the silver moonlight of the castle park, where he soon spied the fairy deer. Together they vanished into the night.

Thomas Rymer was never seen again by humankind. But his prophecies are still remembered.

GOLD-TREE AND
SILVER-TREE

Joseph Jacobs

Once upon a time there was a king who had a wife, whose name was Silver-tree, and a daughter, whose name was Gold-tree. On a certain day of the days, Gold-tree and Silver-tree went to a glen, where there was a well, and in it there was a trout.

Said Silver-tree, 'Troutie, bonny little fellow, am not I the most beautiful queen in the world?'

'Oh! indeed you are not.'

'Who then?'

'Why, Gold-tree, your daughter.'

Silver-tree went home, blind with rage. She lay down on the bed, and vowed she would never be well until she could get the heart and the liver of Gold-tree, her daughter, to eat.

At nightfall the King came home, and it was told him that Silver-tree, his wife, was very ill. He went where she was, and asked her what was wrong with her.

'Oh! only a thing which you may heal if you like.'

'Oh! indeed there is nothing at all which I could do for you that I would not do.'

'If I get the heart and the liver of Gold-tree, my daughter, to eat, I shall be well.'

Now it happened about this time that the son of a great king had come from abroad to ask Gold-tree for marrying. The King now agreed to this, and they went abroad.

The King then went and sent his lads to the hunting-hill for a he-goat, and he gave its heart and its liver to his wife to eat; and she rose well and healthy.

A year after this Silver-tree went to the glen, where there was the well in which there was the trout.

'Troutie, bonny little fellow,' said she, 'am not I the most beautiful queen in the world?'

'Oh! indeed you are not.'

'Who then?'

'Why, Gold-tree, your daughter.'

'Oh! well, it is long since she was living. It is a year since I ate her heart and liver.'

'Oh! indeed she is not dead. She is married to a great prince abroad.'

Silver-tree went home, and begged the King to put the long ship in order, and said, 'I am going to see my dear Gold-tree, for it is so long since I saw her.' The long ship was put in order, and they went away.

It was Silver-tree herself that was at the helm, and she steered the ship so well that they were not long at all before they arrived.

The Prince was out hunting on the hills. Gold-tree knew the long ship of her father coming.

'Oh!' said she to the servants, 'my mother is coming, and she will kill me.'

'She shall not kill you at all; we will lock you in a room where she cannot get near you.'

This was done; and when Silver-tree came ashore, she began to cry out:

'Come to meet your own mother, when she comes to see you.' Gold-tree said that she could not, that she was locked in the room, and that she could not get out of it.

'Will you not put out,' said Silver-tree, 'your little finger through the keyhole, so that your own mother may give a kiss to it?'

She put out her little finger, and Silver-tree went and put a poisoned stab in it, and Gold-tree fell dead.

When the Prince came home, and found Gold-tree dead, he was in great sorrow, and when he saw how beautiful she was, he did not bury her at all, but he locked her in a room where nobody would get near her.

In the course of time he married again, and the whole house was under the management of this wife but one room, and he himself always kept the key of that room. On a certain day of the days he forgot to take the key with him, and the second wife got into the room. What did she see there but the most beautiful woman that she ever saw.

She began to turn and try to wake her, and she noticed the poisoned stab in her finger. She took the stab out, and Gold-tree rose alive, as beautiful as she was ever.

At the fall of night the Prince came home from the hunting-hill, looking very downcast.

'What gift,' said his wife, 'would you give me that I could make you laugh?'

'Oh! indeed, nothing could make me laugh, except if Gold-tree were to come alive again.'

'Well, you'll find her alive down there in the room.'

When the Prince saw Gold-tree alive he made great rejoicings, and he began to kiss her, and kiss her, and kiss her. Said the second wife, 'Since she is the first one you had it is better for you to stick to her, and I will go away.'

'Oh! indeed you shall not go away, but I shall have both of you.'

At the end of that year, Silver-tree went again to the glen, where there was the well, in which there was the trout.

'Troutie, bonny little fellow,' said she, 'am not I the most beautiful queen in the world?'

'Oh! indeed you are not.'

'Who then?'

'Why, Gold-tree, your daughter.'

'Oh! well, she is not alive. It is a year since I put the poisoned stab into her finger.'

'Oh! indeed she is not dead at all, at all.'

Silver-tree went home, and begged the King to put the long ship in order, for that she was going to see her dear Gold-tree, as it was so long since she saw her. The long ship was put in order, and they went away. It was Silver-tree herself that was at the helm, and she steered the ship so well that they were not long at all before they arrived.

The Prince was out hunting on the hills. Gold-tree knew her father's ship coming.

'Oh!' said she, 'my mother is coming again, and she will kill me.'

'Not at all,' said the second wife; 'we will go down to meet her.'

Silver-tree came ashore. 'Come down, Gold-tree, love,' said she, 'for your own mother has come to you with a precious drink.'

'It is a custom in this country,' said the second wife, 'that the person who offers a drink takes a draught out of it first.'

Silver-tree put her mouth to it, and the second wife went and struck it so that some of it went down her throat, and she was poisoned and fell dead. They had only to carry her home a dead corpse and bury her.

The Prince and his two wives were long alive after this, pleased and peaceful.

I left them there.

THE MAGIC WALKING-STICK

John Buchan

When Bill came back for mid-term that autumn half he had
before him a complex programme of entertainment. Thomas,
the keeper, whom he revered more than anyone else in the
world, was to take him in the afternoon to try for a duck in
the big marsh called Alemoor. In the evening Hallowe'en
would be celebrated in the nursery with his small brother
Peter, and he would be permitted to sit up after dinner till
ten o'clock. Next day, which was Sunday, would be devoted
to wandering about with Peter, hearing from him all the
appetizing home news, and pouring into his greedy ears the
gossip of the foreign world of school. On Monday morning,
after a walk with the dogs, he was to be driven up to
London, lunch with Aunt Alice, go to a conjuring show, and
then, after a noble tea, return to school in time for lock-up.

It seemed to Bill all that could be desired in the way of
excitement. But he did not know just how exciting that mid-
term was destined to be.

The first shadow of a cloud appeared after luncheon,

when he had changed into his hunting gear, and Peter and the dogs were waiting at the gunroom door. Bill could not find his own proper stick. It was a long hazel staff, given him by the second stalker in a Scottish deer-forest the year before – a staff rather taller than Bill, of glossy hazel, with a shapely polished crook, and without a ferrule, like all stalking-sticks. He hunted for it high and low, but it could not be found. Without it in his hand Bill felt that an expedition lacked something vital, and he was not prepared to take instead one of his father's shooting-sticks, as Groves, the butler, recommended. Nor would he accept a knobbly cane proffered by Peter. Feeling a little aggrieved and imperfectly equipped, he rushed out to join Thomas. He would cut himself an ash-plant in the first hedge.

But as the two ambled down the lane which led to Alemoor, they came on an old man sitting under a horn-beam. He was a funny little wizened old man, in a shabby long green overcoat, which had once been black, and he wore on his head the oldest and tallest and greenest bowler hat that ever graced a human head. Thomas walked on as if he did not see him, and Gyp, the spaniel, and Shawn, the Irish setter, at the sight of him dropped their tails between their legs, and remembered an engagement a long way off. But Bill stopped, for he saw that the old man had a bundle under his arm, a bundle of ancient umbrellas and queer ragged sticks.

The old man smiled at him, and he had very bright eyes. He seemed to know what was wanted, for he at once took from his bundle a stick. You would not have said that it was the kind of stick Bill was looking for. It was short, and heavy, and made of some dark foreign wood, and instead of a crook it had a handle shaped like a crescent, cut out of some white substance which was neither bone nor ivory. Yet Bill, as soon as he saw it, felt that it was the one stick in the world for him.

'How much?' he asked.

'One penny,' said the old man, and his voice squeaked like a winter wind in a chimney.

Now a penny is not a common price for anything nowadays, but Bill happened to have one – a gift from Peter on his arrival that day, along with a brass cannon, five empty cartridges, a broken microscope, and a badly-printed, brightly-illustrated narrative called *Two Villains Foiled*. But a penny sounded too little, so Bill proffered one of his rare pounds.

'I said one penny,' said the old man rather snappily.

The small coin changed hands, and the little old wizened face seemed to light up with an elfish glee. ''Tis a fine stick, young sir', he squeaked, 'a noble stick, when you gets used to the ways of it.'

Bill had to run to catch up Thomas, who was plodding along with the dogs, now returned from their engagement.

'That's a queer chap – the old stick-man, I mean,' he said.

'I ain't seen no old man, Maaster Bill,' said Thomas. 'What be 'ee talkin' about?'

'The fellow back there. I bought this stick off him.'

Thomas cast a puzzled glance at the stick. 'That be a craafty stick, Maaster Bill –' but he said no more, for Bill had shaken it playfully at the dogs. As soon as they saw it they set off to keep another engagement – this time, apparently, with a hare – and Thomas was yelling and whistling for ten minutes before he brought them to heel.

It was a soft grey afternoon, and Bill was stationed beside one of the deep dykes in the moor, well in cover of a thorn bush, while Thomas and the dogs went off on a long circuit to show themselves beyond the big mere, so that the duck might move in Bill's direction. It was rather cold, and very wet underfoot, for a lot of rain had fallen in the past week, and the mere, which was usually only a sedgy pond, had now grown to a great expanse of shallow flood-water. Bill began his vigil in high excitement. He drove his new stick into the ground, and used the handle as a seat, while he rested his gun in the orthodox way in the crook of his arm. It was a double-barrelled, sixteen bore, and Bill knew that he would be lucky if he got a duck with it; but a duck was to him a bird of mystery, true wild game, and he preferred the chance of one duck to the certainty of many rabbits.

The minutes passed, the grey afternoon sky darkened towards twilight, but no duck came. Bill saw a wedge of geese high up in the sky and longed to salute them; also he heard snipe, but could not locate them in the dim weather. Far away he thought he detected the purring noise which Thomas made to stir the duck, but no overhead beat of wings followed. Soon the mood of eager anticipation died away, and he grew bored and rather despondent. He scrambled up the bank of the dyke and strained his eyes over the moor between the bare boughs of the thorn. He thought he saw duck moving – yes, he was certain of it – they were coming from the direction of Thomas and the dogs. It was perfectly clear what was happening. There was far too much water on the moor, and the birds, instead of flying across the mere to the boundary slopes, were simply settling on the flood. From the misty grey water came the rumour of many wildfowl.

Bill came back to his wet stand grievously disappointed. He did not dare to leave it in case a flight did appear, but he had lost all hope. He tried to warm his feet by moving them up and down in the squelchy turf. His gun was now under his arm, and he was fiddling idly with the handle of the stick which was still embedded in earth. He made it revolve, and as it turned he said aloud: 'I wish I was in the middle of the big flood.'

Then a remarkable thing happened. Bill was not conscious of any movement, but suddenly his surroundings were completely changed. He had still his gun under his left arm and the stick in his right hand, but instead of standing on wet turf he was up to the waist in water . . . And all around him were duck – shovellers, pintail, mallard, teal, widgeon, pochard, tufted – and bigger things that might be geese – swimming or diving or just alighting from the air. In a second Bill realized that his wish had been granted. He was in the very middle of the flood water.

He got a right and left at mallards, missing with his first barrel. Then the birds rose in alarm, and he shoved in fresh cartridges and fired wildly into the air. His next two shots were at longer range, but he was certain that he had hit something. And then the duck vanished in the brume, and he was left alone with the grey waters running out to the dimness.

He lifted up his voice and shouted wildly for Thomas and the dogs, and looked about him to retrieve what he had shot. He had got two anyhow – a mallard drake and a young teal, and he collected them. Presently he heard whistling and splashing, and Gyp the spaniel appeared half swimming, half wading. Gyp picked up a second mallard, and Bill left it at that. He thought he knew roughly where the deeper mere lay so as to avoid it, and with his three duck he started for where he believed Thomas to be. The water was often up to his armpits and once he was soused over his head, and it was a very wet, breathless and excited boy that presently confronted the astounded keeper.

'Where in goodness ha' ye been, Maaster Bill? Them ducks was tigglin' out to the deep water and I was feared ye wouldn't get a shot. Three on 'em, no less! My word, ye 'ave poonished 'em.'

'I was in the deep water,' said Bill, but he explained no more, for it had just occurred to him that he couldn't. It was a boy not less puzzled than triumphant that returned to show his bag to his family, and at dinner he was so abstracted that his mother thought he was ill and sent him early to bed. Bill made no complaint, for he wanted to be alone to think things out.

It was plain that a miracle had happened, and it must be connected with the stick. He had wished himself in the middle of the flood-water – he remembered that clearly – and at the time he had been doing something to the stick. What was it? It had been stuck in the ground, and he had been playing with the handle. Yes, that was it. He had been turning it round when he uttered the wish. Bill's mind was better stored with fairy-tales than with Latin and Greek, and he remembered many precedents. The stick was in the rack in the hall, and he had half a mind to slip downstairs and see if he could repeat the performance. But he reflected that he might be observed, and that this was a business demanding profound secrecy. So he resolutely composed himself to sleep. He had been allowed for a treat to have his old bed in the night-nursery, next to Peter, and he realized that he must be up bright and early to frustrate that alert young inquirer.

*

He woke before dawn, and at once put on socks and shoes and a dressing-gown, and tiptoed downstairs. He heard a housemaid moving in the direction of the dining-room, and Groves opening the library shutters, but the hall was deserted. He groped in the rack and found the stick, struggled with the key of the garden door, and emerged into the foggy winter half-light. It was very cold, as he padded down the lawn to a shrubbery beside the pond, and his shoes were soon soaked with hoar-frost. He shivered and drew his dressing-gown around him, but he had decided what to do. In this kind of weather he wished to be warm. He planted his stick in the turf.

'I want to be on the beach in the Solomon Islands,' said Bill, and three times twisted the handle.

In a second his eyes seemed to dazzle with excess of light and something beat on his body like a blast from an open furnace ... He was standing on an expanse of blinding white sand at which a lazy blue sea was licking. Behind him at a distance of perhaps two hundred yards was a belt of high green forest, out of which stuck a tall crest of palms. A hot wind was blowing and tossing the tree-tops, but it only crisped the sea.

Bill gasped with joy to find his dream realized. He was in the far Pacific where he had always longed to be ... But he was very hot, and could not endure the weight of winter pyjamas and winter dressing-gown. Also he longed to bathe in those inviting waters. So he shed everything and hopped gaily down to the tide's edge, leaving the stick still upright in the sand.

The sea was as delicious as it looked, but Bill, though a good swimmer, kept near the edge for fear of sharks. He wallowed and splashed, with the fresh salt smell which he loved in his nostrils. Minutes passed rapidly, and he was just on the point of striking out for a little reef, when he cast a glance towards the shore ...

At the edge of the forest stood men – dark-skinned men, armed with spears.

Bill scrambled to his feet with a fluttering heart, and as he rose the men moved forward. He was, perhaps, fifty yards from the stick, which cast its long morning shadow on the sand, and they were two hundred yards on the farther side. At all costs he must get there first. He sprang out of the sea, and as he ran he saw to his horror that the men ran also – ran in great bounds – shouting and brandishing their spears.

Those fifty yards seemed miles, but Bill won the race. No time to put on his clothes. He seized his dressing-gown with one hand and the stick with the other, and as he twirled the handle a spear whizzed by his ear. 'I want to be home,' he gasped, and the next second he stood naked between the shrubbery and the pond, clutching his dressing-gown. The Solomon Islands had got his shoes and his pyjamas.

The cold of a November morning brought him quickly to his senses. He clothed his shivering body in his dressing-gown and ran by devious paths to the house. Happily the gunroom door was unlocked, and he was able to ascend by way of empty passages and back stairs to the nursery floor. He did not, however, escape the eagle eye of Elsie, the nurse, who read the riot act over a boy who went out of doors imperfectly clad on such a morning. She prophesied pneumonia, and plumped him into a hot bath.

Bill applied his tongue to the back of his hand. Yes. It tasted salt, and the salt smell was still in his nose. It had not been a dream . . . He hugged himself in the bath and made strange gurgling sounds of joy. Life had suddenly opened up for him in dazzling vistas of adventure.

His conduct in church that morning was exemplary, for while Peter at his side had his usual Sunday attack of St Vitus's Dance, Bill sat motionless as a mummy. On the way home his mother commented on it and observed that he seemed to have learned how to behave. But his thoughts during the service had not been devotional. The stick lay beside him on the floor, and for a moment he had a wild notion of twisting it during the sermon and disappearing for a few minutes to Kamchatka. Then prudence supervened. He must go very cautiously in this business, and court no questions. That afternoon he and Peter would seek a secluded spot and make experiments. He would take the stick back to school and hide it in his room – he had a qualm when he thought what a blunder it would be if a boy from the lower school appeared with it in public! For him no more hours of boredom. School would no longer be a place of exile, but a rapturous holiday. He would slip home now and then and see what was happening – he would go often to Glenmore – he would visit any spot in the globe which took his fancy. His imagination reeled at the prospect, and he cloaked his chortles of delight in a fervent Amen.

At luncheon it was decided that Peter and he should go for a walk together, and should join the others at a place called the Roman Camp. 'Let the boys have a chance of being alone,' his father had said. This exactly suited Bill's book, and as they left the dining-room he clutched his small brother. 'Shrimp,' he said in his ear, 'You're going to have the afternoon of your life.'

It was a mild, grey day, with the leafless woods and the brown ploughlands lit by a pale November sun. Peter, as he trotted beside him, jerked out breathless inquiries about what Bill proposed to do, and was told to wait and see.

Arriving at a clump of beeches which promised privacy, Bill first swore his brother to secrecy by the most awful oaths which he could imagine.

'Put your arm round my waist and hang on to my belt,' he told him. 'I'm going to take you to have a look at Glenmore.'

'Don't be silly,' said Peter. 'That only happens in summer, and we haven't packed yet.'

'Shut up and hold tight,' said Bill as he twirled the stick and spoke the necessary words . . .

The boys were looking not at the smooth boles of beeches, but at a little coppice of rowans and birches above the narrow glen of the hill burn. It was Glenmore in very truth. There was the strip of mossy lawn, the whitewashed gable end of the lodge; there to the left beside the walled garden was the smoking chimney of the keeper's cottage; there beyond the trees was the long lift of brown moorland and the blue top of Stob Ghabhar. To the boys Glenmore was the true home of the soul, but they had seen it only in the glory of late summer and early autumn. In its winter dress it seemed for a moment strange. Then the sight of an old collie waddling across the lawn gave the connecting link.

'There's Wattie,' Peter gasped, and lifted up his voice in an excited summons. His brother promptly made to throttle him.

'Don't be an ass, Shrimp,' he said fiercely. 'This is a secret, you fat-head. This is magic. Nobody must know we are here. Come on and explore.'

For an hour – it must have been an hour, Bill calculated afterwards, but it seemed like ten minutes – the two visited their favourite haunts. They found the robbers' cave in the glen where a raven nested, and the pool where Bill had caught his first pound trout, and the stretch in the river where their father that year had had the thirty-pound salmon. There were no blaeberries or crowberries in the woods, but there were many woodcock, and Bill had a shot with his catapult at a wicked old blackcock on a peat-stack. Also they waylaid Wattie, the collie, and induced him to make a third in the party. All their motions were as stealthy as an Indian's, and the climax of the adventure was reached when they climbed the garden wall and looked in at the window of the keeper's cottage.

Tea was laid before a bright peat fire in the parlour, so Mrs Macrae must be expecting company. It looked a very good tea, for there were scones and pancakes, and shortbread and currant-loaf and heather honey. Both boys felt suddenly famished at the sight.

'Mrs Macrae always gives me a scone and honey,' Peter bleated. 'I'm hungry. I want one.'

So did Bill. His soul longed for food, but he kept hold of his prudence.

'We daren't show ourselves,' he whispered. 'But, perhaps, we might pinch a scone. It wouldn't be stealing, for if Mrs Macrae saw us she would say "Come awa in, laddies, and get a jeely piece." I'll give you a back, Shrimp, and in you get.'

The window was open, and Peter was hoisted through, falling with a bang on a patchwork rug. But he never reached the table, for at that moment the parlour door opened and someone entered. After that things happened fast. Peter, urged by Bill's anguished whisper, turned back to the window, and was hauled through by the scruff of the neck. A woman's voice was heard crying, 'Mercy on us, it's the bairns,' as the culprits darted to the shelter of the gooseberry bushes.

Bill realized that there was no safety in the garden, so he dragged Peter over the wall by the way they had come, thereby seriously damaging a pear tree. But they had been observed, and as they scrambled out of a rose-bed, they heard cries and saw Mrs Macrae appearing round the end of the wall, having come through the stable yard. Also a figure, which looked like Angus, the river gillie, was running from the same direction.

There was nothing for it but to go. Bill seized Peter with one hand and the stick with the other, and spoke the words, with Angus not six yards away . . . As he looked once more at the familiar beech boles, his ears were still full of the cries of an excited woman and the frenzied howling of Wattie, the dog.

The two boys, very warm and flustered and rather

scratched about the hands and legs, confronted their father and mother and their sister, Barbara, who was sixteen and very proud.

'Hullo, hullo,' they heard their father say. 'I thought you'd be hiding somewhere hereabouts. You young rascals know how to take cover, for you seemed to spring out of the ground. You look as if you'd been playing football. Better walk home with us and cool down . . . Bless my soul, Peter, what's that you've got? It's bog myrtle! Where on earth did you find it? I've never seen it before in Oxfordshire.'

Then Barbara raised a ladylike voice. 'Oh, Mummy, look at the mess they've made of themselves. They've been among the brambles, for Peter has two holes in his socks. Just look at Bill's hands!' And she wrinkled her finical nose, and sniffed.

Bill kept a diplomatic silence, and Peter, usually garrulous, did the same, for his small wrist was in his brother's savage clutch.

That night, before Peter went to bed, he was compelled once more to swear solemn oaths, and Bill was so abstracted that his mother thought that he was sickening for some fell disease. He lay long awake, planning out the best way to use his marvellous new possession. His thoughts were still on the subject next morning, and to his family's amazement he made no protest when, to suit his mother's convenience, it was decided to start for London soon after breakfast, and the walk with the dogs was cancelled. He departed in high spirits, most unlike his usual leave-takings, and his last words to Peter were fierce exhortations to secrecy.

All the way to London he was in a happy dream, and at luncheon he was so urbane that Aunt Alice, who had strong and unorthodox views about education, announced that in Bill's case, at any rate, the public school system seemed to answer, and gave him double her customary tip.

Then came the conjuring show at the Grafton Hall. Bill in the past had had an inordinate appetite for such entertainments, and even in his new ecstasy he looked forward to this one. But at the door of the hall he had a shock. Hitherto he had kept close to his stick, but it was now necessary to give it up and receive a metal check for it. To his mother's surprise he protested hotly. 'It won't do any harm,' he pleaded. 'It will stay beside me under the seat.' But the rule was inexorable and he had to surrender it. 'Don't be afraid, darling,' his mother told him. 'That funny new stick of yours won't be lost. The check is a receipt for it, and they are very careful.'

The show was not up to his expectations. What were all these disappearing donkeys and vanishing ladies compared to the performances he had lately staged? Bill was puffed up with a great pride. With the help of his stick he could make rings round this trumpery cleverness. He was the true magician . . . He wished that the thing would end that he might feel the precious stick again in his hand.

At the counter there was no sign of the man who had given him the check. Instead there was a youth who seemed to be new to the business, and who was very slow in returning the sticks and umbrellas. When it came to Bill's turn he was extra slow, and presently announced that he could find no Number 229.

Bill's mother, seeing his distress, intervened, and sent the wretched youth to look again, while other people were kept waiting, but he came back with the same story. There was no duplicate Number 229, or any article to correspond to the check. After that he had to be allowed to attend to the others, and Bill, almost in tears, waited hysterically till the crowd had gone. Then there was a thorough search, and Bill and his mother were allowed to go behind the counter. But no Number 229 could be found, and there were no sticks left, only three umbrellas.

Bill was now patently in tears.

'Never mind, darling,' his mother said, 'we must be off now, or you will be late for lock-up. I promise that your father will come here tomorrow and clear up the whole business. Never fear – the stick will be found.'

But it is still lost.

When Bill's father went there next day, and cross-examined the wretched youth – for he had once been a barrister – he extracted a curious story. If the walking-stick was lost, so also was the keeper of the walking-sticks, for the youth was only an assistant. The keeper – his name was Jukes and he lived in Hammersmith – had not been seen since yesterday afternoon during the performance, and Mrs Jukes had come round and made a scene last night, and that morning the police had been informed. Mr Jukes, it appeared, was not a very pleasant character, and he had had too much beer at luncheon. When the audience had all gone in, he had been telling his assistant how fed up he was. The youth's testimony ran as follows: 'Mr Jukes, 'e was wavin' his arm something chronic and carryin' on about 'ow this was no billet for a man like 'im. He picks up a stick, and I thought he was goin' to 'it me. "Percy, me lad," says 'e, "I'm fed up – fed up to the back teeth." He starts twisting the stick, and says 'e, "I wish to 'eaven I was out of 'ere." After that I must 'ave come over faint, for when I looks again, 'e 'ad 'opped it.'

Mr Jukes' case is still a puzzle to Mrs Jukes and the police, but Bill understands only too clearly what happened. Mr Jukes and the stick have gone 'out of 'ere,' and where that may be neither Bill nor I can guess.

But Bill lives in hope, and he wants me to broadcast this story in case the stick may have come back to earth. So let every boy and girl keep a sharp eye on shops where sticks are sold. The magic walking-stick is not quite four feet long, and about one inch and a quarter thick. It is made of a heavy dark-red wood, rather like the West Indian purple-heart. Its handle is in the shape of a crescent with the horns uppermost, made of some white substance which is neither bone nor ivory. If anyone sees such a stick, then Bill will give all his worldly wealth for news of it.

Failing that, he would like information about the man who sold it to him. He is very old, small and wizened, but his eyes are the brightest you ever saw in a human head. He wears a shabby, greeny-black overcoat which reaches down to his heels, and a tall, greeny-black bowler hat. It is possible that the stick may have returned to him. So if you meet anyone like him, look sharply at his bundle, and if it is there and he is willing to sell, *buy it – buy it – buy it*, or you will regret it all your days. For this purpose it is wise always to have a penny in your pocket, for he won't take anything else.

Part Two

GIANTS AND MONSTERS

THE TWO SHEPHERDS

J. F. Campbell

There were living in the country between Lochaber and Badenoch two shepherds who were neighbours to each other, and the one would often visit the other. One lived on the east side of the River Spean, and the other lived on the west. One evening, the one from the west side came to visit the one on the east side. He stayed till it was pretty late, and then he wished to go home.

'It's time I was going home,' said he.

'It's far too late, you can just stay here tonight,' said the other.

'I can't stay; the only bother is crossing the river, and once I'm over that, I'll be fine,' said the first man.

The host had a big, strong son, who said, 'If you insist on going home, I'll go with you, and see you safe over the river. But my father's right – you'd be better staying here for what's left of the night.'

'No, I must get back.'

'In that case, I'll go with you,' said the lad, who called his dog to accompany them.

When he had seen their visitor safe across the river, he set out to wade back over the water, carrying his boots and stockings in one hand. Suddenly the dog, which had been swimming alongside him quite happily, made a great splashing leap into the arms of the shepherd lad. Not wanting to get soaked, he threw her off, scolding her for wetting him. Thus they came back to their own side of the river. Then the shepherd lad noticed that he had somehow mislaid his hat. 'What a nuisance,' he said to himself. 'Did I lose it in the river when the dog jumped up, or did I leave it on the far side? I can't go home without my good hat.' So, for the third time that night, he crossed the river and soon saw, on the far bank, a big man seated right where he had said good night to his father's friend, and holding his bonnet in his hand. Now, as we said, the shepherd lad was a big, brawny, muscular boy, and fearlessly he went straight up to the big man. Catching hold of the bonnet, he took it from him.

'What business have you with that?' the lad asked. 'It belongs to me.' And putting the hat firmly on his head, he turned and made to cross the river for the fourth time that night. But the big man came after him, and put his arm under the arm of the shepherd lad, and began to drag him down into one of the deep pools of the river. The shepherd lad defended himself, and fought back bravely, wondering who on earth this silent stranger could be, and why he should wish to attack him. He felt himself losing his footing, and stretched his arm up to grip the branch of an oak tree which hung out over the water. But the big man was striving hard to pull the lad down into the water, and the shepherd's son could feel the tree start to give way and creak over towards the water. He panicked just a little then, as he heard the roots loosening and giving way on the riverbank. Just when he felt the last root give way, and he thought that all was lost, he heard the cocks crow in his father's farmyard. Then the shepherd lad realized that it was almost daybreak, for he saw a gleam of yellowish light in the eastern sky.

The big man had also heard the cocks crowing, and said to the lad, 'You've stood your ground well, son, and you're a bonny fechter. That's just as well, and you needed to defend yourself – or your bonnet would have cost you dear!' Then the big man left the scene, and has never been seen again from that day to this.

THE SPRIGHTLY TAILOR

Joseph Jacobs

A sprightly tailor was employed by the great Macdonald, in his castle at Saddell in Kintyre, in order to make the laird a pair of trews, as used in olden time. And trews being the vest and breeches united in one piece, and ornamented with fringes, were very comfortable, and suitable to be worn in walking or dancing. And Macdonald had said to the tailor as a sort of a dare, that if he would make the trews by night in the church, he would get a handsome reward. For it was thought that the old ruined church was haunted, and that fearsome things were to be seen there at night.

The tailor was well aware of this; but he was a sprightly man, and when the laird dared him to make the trews by night in the church, the tailor was not to be daunted, but took it in hand to gain the prize. So, when night came, away he went up the glen, about half a mile's distance from the castle, till he came to the old church. Then he chose him a nice gravestone for a seat and he lighted his candle, and put on his thimble, and set to work at the trews; plying his

needle nimbly, and thinking about the prize that the laird
would have to give him.

For some time he got on pretty well, until he felt the floor
all of a tremble under his feet; and looking about him, but
keeping his fingers at work, he saw the appearance of a
massive human head rising up through the stone pavement
of the church. And when the head had risen above the
surface, there came from it a great, great voice. And the
voice said: 'Do you see this great head of mine?'

'I see that, but I'll sew this!' replied the sprightly tailor;
and he kept stitching away at the trews.

Then the head rose higher up through the pavement, until its
neck appeared. And when its neck was shown, the thundering
voice came again and said: 'Do you see this great neck of mine?'

'I see that, but I'll sew this!' said the sprightly tailor; and
he kept stitching away at his trews.

Then the head and neck rose higher still, until the great
shoulders and chest were shown above the ground. And

again the mighty voice thundered: 'Do you see this great chest of mine?'

And again the sprightly tailor replied: 'I see that, but I'll sew this!' and he kept stitching away at his trews.

And still the monster kept rising through the pavement, until it shook a great pair of arms in the tailor's face, and said: 'Do you see these great arms of mine?'

'I see those, but I'll sew this!' answered the tailor; and he kept stitching hard at his trews, for he knew that he had no time to lose.

The sprightly tailor was doing the long stitches, when he saw the monster gradually rising and rising through the floor, until it lifted out a great leg, and stamping with it upon the pavement, said in a roaring voice: 'Do you see this great leg of mine?'

'Aye, aye: I see that, but I'll sew this!' cried the tailor; and his fingers flew with the needle, and he made such long stitches, that he was just coming to the end of the trews, when the monster was taking up its other leg. But before it could pull it out of the pavement, the sprightly tailor had finished his task; and, blowing out his candle, and springing from off his gravestone, he buckled up his coat, and ran out of the church with the trews under his arm. Then the fearsome thing gave a loud roar, and stamped with both his feet upon the pavement, and out of the church he went thundering after the sprightly tailor.

Down the glen they ran, faster than the stream when the flood rides it; but the tailor had got the start and a nimble pair of legs, and he did not choose to lose the laird's reward. And though the thing roared to him to stop, the sprightly tailor was not the man to be restrained by a monster if he could help it. So he held his trews tight, and let no darkness grow under his feet, until he had reached Saddell Castle. He had no sooner got inside the gate, and shut it, than the monster came up to it; and, enraged at losing his prize, struck the wall above the gate, and left there the mark of his five great fingers. You may see them plainly to this day, if you'll only peer close enough.

But the sprightly tailor gained his reward: for Macdonald was impressed by his courage and paid him handsomely for the trews, and never discovered that a few of the stitches were somewhat long.

THE LONELY GIANT

Alasdair MacLean

There was a giant once who was lonely. Most giants are, of
course, or would be if they stopped to think about it. A
giant needs a great deal of land to live off, which means that
giants have to space themselves out very thinly, something
like one to every shire. So the only time they see one another
is on the rare occasions when two neighbouring giants
happen to arrive at the borders of their territories at the
same time. When that takes place they usually play catch for
a time with a boulder or have a game of hide-and-seek
among the mountains. Then they go their separate ways.
You can hear them shouting goodbye for miles.

They don't think about this loneliness, however, because
thinking isn't something they go in for very much. Mostly
they just get on with the business of being giants, which
takes up all their time and which is very hard work because
it is laid down in the Rule Book for Giants that, when they
aren't actually eating or sleeping, they have to stamp around
the countryside bellowing at the tops of their voices and

looking very fierce. Looking fierce is hard work in itself as you'll find out if you try it for half an hour. You keep forgetting that you're supposed to have a scowl on your face and you find yourself smiling at something. Then you have to start all over again.

Being kept so busy means that giants don't have much time for thinking. When a giant does manage to get a few minutes to himself he generally feels so tired that he just drops off to sleep. He sits down first of all with his back against the nearest hill. Then he opens his huge mouth and gives a huge yawn. Then he spits out all the birds that have got sucked into his mouth while the yawn was going on. Then off he goes to dream-land.

But the giant who was lonely was different. He had long since lost his rule book and had never bothered to get it replaced. He didn't go around stamping and roaring because he couldn't see much point in it. It only made your feet sore and gave you a headache. Besides that, it frightened people away and he didn't want to frighten people away. He wanted to be friendly.

What made him especially different from other giants, though, was that he was always thinking, and what he was always thinking about was how much alone he was. It was true that he did have one or two friends among the creatures. There was Goldentop, the eagle, for example. But the creatures as a rule weren't greatly interested in people big or little, considering them a very limited species incapable of running at much more than a trot, or swimming farther than a few miles, or flying any higher than five or six feet and staying up any longer than one or two seconds, or burrowing underground, or carrying their houses on their backs or anything really worthwhile like that.

'As for people,' said Goldentop once to the lonely giant – whose name, by the way, was Angus Macaskill – 'all that they are good for, whether they are big or little and with very few exceptions, is making a noise or making places dirty or breaking things. And all that pink naked skin on them without a single feather! Ugh!' So all that Angus got from Goldentop, usually, was a dip of the wings in passing.

It was true, also, that Angus did have one or two friends among the ordinary-sized folk. There was Morag Matheson, for instance, the shoemaker's daughter. He sometimes had quite good conversations with her. But in order for them to talk either Angus had to lie down to get his ear to the level of her mouth, which usually struck him as such a comical proceeding that he burst into fits of laughter, or he had to pick her up and hold her to his ear, which usually struck her as such a comical proceeding that she burst into fits of laughter.

It is difficult, as you will know from your own experience, to have a sensible talk with someone who giggles all the time. You can hear properly only one or two words in every sentence and you have to guess at the rest. If you guess wrongly, of course, it produces even more laughter. Morag had once told Angus that her mother had been ordered by the doctor to eat two legs for breakfast every day. He was quite horrified till he discovered that she had really said 'eggs'.

One day Angus's loneliness became more than he could bear and he realized that he would have to do something about it. He thought that the wisest thing he could do would be to ask for advice and he decided to ask Morag first of all. He went along to her father's house and saw her in the distance, as he approached, sitting at the front door, spinning and singing, the sound and the thread flowing out with equal sweetness.

I wish I were not a giant, thought Angus, *then I could ask Morag to marry me. And if she said 'Yes' I would not be lonely any more.*

But he *was* a giant, therefore he put that thought away

from him, as a peasant lad might put away a thought of the king's daughter. Instead, he picked Morag up so quickly that she was too much out of breath to start laughing.

'Morag,' he said, 'listen to me carefully because I need your advice. And don't laugh, please, because it's a very serious matter. The trouble is that I am lonely. What can I do about it? Is there any cure?'

'I wish you weren't a giant,' Morag answered. 'Or I wish that I were. I would soon cure your loneliness.'

'How?' asked Angus.

'Never mind,' replied Morag. She thought long and hard and sadly. 'The only cure for you, Angus,' she said at last, 'is to get married. You must find yourself a giantess somewhere.'

'Where?' asked Angus.

'Well, now, that I don't know,' Morag answered. 'Most of the people I have met in my life have been very small in one way or another. You'd better ask Goldentop the eagle. He's always boasting that he knows every mountain in the whole Land of Lorne.'

'Giants aren't mountains,' Angus pointed out.

'No,' agreed Morag. 'Giants are lighter coloured and more gentle. At least, some of them are.' She looked at the ground, where it dizzied away into the distance. 'But there are certain resemblances just the same.'

Angus in his turn looked down at the ground. Somewhere down there were daisies and primroses and violets. 'Yes,' he sighed. 'I know what you mean.' He put Morag down very gently and set off in search of Goldentop.

The eagle was sat on a favourite perch. One of his eyes was watching the approach of Angus and it was more or less blank. The other was fixed on some hills that stuck up above the horizon and it was a calculating eye, the sort of eye that added up figures and got one less every time.

'What are you watching with that left eye?' asked Angus.

'A flock of sheep leaving Hugh Henderson's sheep-fold in the village of Carraig in the parish of Cray,' answered Goldentop.

'You have good eyesight,' said Angus.

'I have an empty belly,' said the eagle. 'It clears the vision of trivialities.'

'Has this vision of yours ever rested on a giantess?' queried Angus. 'An unattached one, I mean.'

'Island of Alva,' replied Goldentop promptly. 'Walk north along the coast till you come to the Blue Bay. Then swim due west.'

'Ah, but are you sure she's unattached?' insisted Angus. 'There might have been a giant there when you weren't looking.'

'Somehow I do not think so,' remarked the eagle thoughtfully.

'Anyway, I can't go to this island,' Angus told him, 'even if I could swim that far. My mother told me on her deathbed never to go into the salt water.'

'Then you must balance the commands of the dead against the requirements of the living,' said Goldentop. 'It is an old dilemma. But not for eagles.' He left the perch and slid upwards, heading in the direction of the sheep.

Angus didn't know what to do. He decided that while he was making up his mind he might as well walk to the Blue Bay. He had never been there and it sounded like a pleasant spot. Besides, he knew that there is nothing like a good long walk for getting rid of sadness. It flows out of your feet into the ground, which of course is where it comes from in the first place, only it enters through your bottom while you are sitting down.

By the time he reached the Blue Bay he was feeling a lot better. He knew it was the right place because the surrounding hills were blue and the sea was blue and the sky was blue. Also there was a small stunted signpost near by, growing crookedly between two rocks, and on it there said in blue letters, *This is the Blue Bay*.

The tide was out when he got there. Indeed it was so far out that it might well need the help of a signpost itself to get back. It had left behind it, as a pledge perhaps, a mile or more of ribbed sand and stranded right in the middle of this sand there was a whale. If you think it was anything other than a blue whale you have not been following my story as closely as you should.

Angus approached the whale circumspectly, which means that he stopped about fifty feet away. He could see that it had worn a hollow in the sand by threshing around. When it saw him it shouted 'Help!' in a tiny squeaky voice, whales having very small throats.

'What seems to be the trouble, Whale?' inquired Angus.

'The trouble, Giant,' replied the whale, 'is that I fell asleep on a sandbank in the middle of the bay. It was only a baby sandbank then but by the time I woke it had grown up. I am stranded. Unless I can get back to the water soon this hot white sun will shrivel my tender skin, which is used only to the coolness and moistness and greenness of the deep sea. I shall die. But what can I do? I cannot swim over the sand and I have neither legs to walk with nor wings to fly.'

It was plain that he spoke the truth, for already on his blue back two or three blisters were beginning to form.

'It seems to me,' remarked Angus, 'that you creatures aren't quite as superior as Goldentop is always saying you are. I may be only a giant but at least I would never get stuck in the middle of a flat piece of land. I have legs.'

'Goldentop is a snob,' said the whale. 'It comes of continually looking down on the rest of the world. And as for legs, unless they are put to the service of the community they remain a private luxury.'

'You are a heavy weight,' Angus told him. 'Even for me. But I think that with the help of my legs – and arms – I might just be able to pull you as far as the water's edge.'

He caught hold of the whale's tail and set to work. After

a long hard struggle he managed to get it into the shallows, and with a flick of its powerful body it did the rest. It was so happy to be back where it belonged that it turned three underwater cart-wheels in succession.

'Look at me, Giant!' it shouted when it re-emerged. 'Where are your legs now? Can you swim like this?'

'I'm afraid I'm not very much of a swimmer,' replied Angus. 'If I were I might swim across to the Island of Alva, for on it there lives a giantess.'

'I know,' said the whale.

'Have you seen her?' Angus asked.

'I have seen her,' the whale agreed. 'And heard her too.'

'I am going to ask her to marry me,' Angus informed him.

'Have *you* seen her?' inquired the whale.

'No,' replied Angus. 'Why do you ask?'

'Never mind,' the whale answered. 'But I owe my life to you and if you truly wish to go there I will help you. Wade into the water and catch hold of my tail.'

'It's very kind of you,' Angus told him. 'But there's one more snag. My mother told me just before she died never to go into the sea.'

'And died, I suppose,' asked the whale, 'before she had time to say why?' Angus nodded. 'That's the trouble with Death,' the whale continued. 'He always comes when you're in the middle of something, even if it's only drawing breath. Well, it's up to you whether you want to take a chance or not. I'll give you five minutes to make up your mind.'

The whale set off on a slow tour round the bay, or what was left of it. Angus pondered. What was the mysterious salt-water fate that lay in store for giants? Was it some monster of the deep? Something big enough to swallow even him? And whatever the fate was could it be any worse than loneliness?

The sea looked lovely. Surely nothing too terrible could happen to him if he ventured in? There was the Giantess, too, to think about, on her island just below the horizon.

Very likely she was waiting impatiently for just such a one as he was. He decided to take the risk.

'I'm going to the island!' he shouted to the whale. 'I'm ready now!'

They began their voyage, with Angus grasping the tail of his new friend and being towed through the water. Their progress, to be sure, was slow, for a giant is a considerable burden even for a whale. But the sun shone, the sea remained peaceful, no monsters appeared and one by one the miles slid past beneath them. Gradually they began to go a little faster.

Angus noticed this. 'You're getting used to me!' he called.

'I expect that's it,' the whale agreed.

On they went a mile or two farther and still the sea unrolled quietly before them like a great blue carpet. Their speed increased a little more.

Angus noticed this as well. 'Wonderful!' he shouted. 'You're going faster than ever!'

'I'm not sure that I am,' the whale said. 'There's something very strange going on. I don't understand it at all.' He sounded worried.

On they went again. Faster and still faster. Angus noticed that his hands didn't grasp the whale's tail as easily as they had when he started. 'That's because of the speed,' he told himself. But almost as soon as he said it he knew it wasn't true. His mother's warning sounded again in his ears. 'Don't go into the salt water, Angus!' And suddenly he realized what she had meant. He was slowly shrinking!

What could he do? He called out once more to his friend the whale, telling it what was happening.

'Yes, I thought you must be getting smaller,' the whale admitted. 'But I was afraid to say anything in case you dropped off through shock.'

'Should we turn back?' asked Angus.

'We're there,' replied the whale. Sure enough, the island loomed ahead, a large well-wooded one with the tallest tower that Angus had ever seen soaring above the tree-tops.

'That'll be the Giantess's tower, I suppose,' thought Angus. The island grew nearer and nearer and presently a great booming voice thundered out across the water.

> *I am a giant, a female giant,*
> *by nature bold and strong.*
> *My eyes are quick, my club is thick,*
> *my arms are extra long.*
>
> *My voice is thunderously large,*
> *a wondrous voice to hear,*
> *and when I shout and stamp about,*
> *the echoes take a year.*
>
> *My towering height is something else*
> *of which I'm very proud.*
> *I scrape the sky when I pass by*
> *and drink from every cloud.*

A tailor who was measuring me
and swore he had the knack,
set off in haste to chalk my waist
and hasn't yet come back.

My future husband, I insist,
must be more huge than me,
or with one bound I'll swing him around
and hurl him out to sea.'

'Grammar never was her strong point,' said the whale, 'but she sounds in excellent form today.'

Angus had listened in trepidation to the great voice and to the awesome catalogue of attributes it had listed. He had tried to give himself courage by allowing ten per cent off the list for the usual giant's exaggeration. But even if she were only half of what she claimed, the Giantess must be a formidable woman indeed. Somehow it was difficult to imagine her darning socks. And apart from that there was the worrying discovery he had made in the sea just now. How much had he shrunk?

The whale glided into the shallow water of the creek. Angus released his hold, waded ashore and turned to face his friend. 'How much have I lost?' he inquired anxiously.

'A lot,' replied the whale, surveying him. 'An awful lot. You've dwindled by about half.'

The voice Angus had heard on approaching the island rolled out again, sounding louder and nearer all the time. He found himself thinking with longing of his home territory and of the clear eyes of Goldentop and the fringed ones of Morag Matheson.

'You know, I think perhaps I'll come back some other time,' he said to the whale. 'I don't feel in the right frame of mind for courting.'

'It's too late to back out now,' the whale told him. 'Here she comes!' He nodded with his head in the direction of

Angus's right shoulder. 'Good luck!' he added and with a flick of his tail he was gone. Angus turned. The 'tower' he had seen above the tree-tops was advancing down the beach towards him. It was the Giantess!

'Good afternoon,' said Angus politely, the occasion obviously being one that called for politeness. The Giantess said nothing but she stooped suddenly and her huge hand shot out. Before he realized what she was about she had grasped him by the waist and swung him up to face level.

'Angus Macaskill is my name,' said Angus hurriedly. 'I'm a giant. At least, I was this morning. I'm from the mainland. I have quite a good little territory over there. Lots of butter and eggs and vegetables and that sort of thing. More than enough for two. I'm looking for a wife, I think. Will you marry me?'

The Giantess listened to this recital in complete silence. When it was finished she spoke just one word. 'Cheek!' she said. The hand that grasped Angus drew back quickly and then shot forward. He found himself flying out over the sea in a huge tumbling curve that arched slowly down towards the waves.

Goodbye, world! he thought. *Goodbye!* And splash! He hit the water. But before he could sink, there beside him was the whale.

'You landed just about where I thought you would,' he said to Angus. 'Hang on and I'll have you back at the Blue Bay in no time.'

Angus spat out a mouthful of salt water. 'If I shrink as much on the way back as I did when I came here,' he said, 'there'll be nothing left of me.'

'I'll go extra specially fast,' the whale promised. And so he did. He tore through the water at such a rate that Angus had to hold on with all his strength. Even so, he felt himself shrinking so much smaller that his clothes began to fall off. He had to clutch them desperately.

When they landed in the Blue Bay they went through the same routine as at the island. 'How much have I lost this time?' Angus asked, after he had waded ashore.

The whale looked him over carefully. 'Well, not as much as last time,' he answered. 'But still quite a lot. You're about ordinary-sized now. I shouldn't try it again.'

'Don't worry,' Angus told him. 'It's dry land for me from now on. Dry land and a bit more reverence for the wisdom of mothers. Thanks for rescuing me.'

'At least you can say one thing,' said the whale.

'What's that?' asked Angus.

'You're not the first man to shrink from courtship,' the whale answered. He dived under the water and vanished.

Angus made his way home as quickly as he could and the first person he went to see was Morag. He found her spinning and singing as before but more slowly and sadly than she used to.

'It's me!' he shouted when he reached her. 'I'm back!'

'Angus?' cried Morag. 'I recognize your voice but where are you?' She was so busy craning her neck skyward that she failed to notice him standing beside her.

'I'm down here,' he told her. 'The salt water shrank me. I'm just about your size now.'

'So you are,' she agreed. Her eyes dropped down from the clouds, rested on him briefly and kept on dropping till her gaze was fixed on the ground.

'Will you marry me, Morag?' he asked.

'Yes, I will,' she replied. So they got married and lived as happily as two people in love might reasonably expect to live. They had three ordinary-sized children, two girls and a boy, none of whom could ever be persuaded to go near the sea. Angus stopped being lonely.

ASSIPATTLE AND THE
MESTER STOORWORM

Elizabeth Grierson

In far bygone days, on the Mainland of Orkney, there lived
a well-to-do farmer, who had seven sons and one daughter.
And the youngest of these seven sons bore a very curious
name; for he was called Assipattle, which means, 'He who
grovels among the ashes'.

Perhaps Assipattle deserved his name, for he was rather a
lazy boy, who never did any work on the farm as his
brothers did, but ran about outdoors with ragged clothes
and unkempt hair, and whose mind was ever filled with
wondrous stories of trolls and giants, elves and goblins.

When the sun was hot in the long summer afternoons, when
the bees droned drowsily and even the tiny insects seemed
almost asleep, the boy was content to throw himself down on
the ash-heap amongst the ashes, and lie there, lazily letting
them run through his fingers, as one might play with sand on the
sea-shore, basking in the sunshine and telling stories to himself.

And his brothers, working hard in the fields, would point

to him with mocking fingers, and laugh, and say to each other how well the name suited him, and how little use he was in the world.

And when they came home from their work, they would push him about and tease him, and even his mother would make him sweep the floor, and draw water from the well, and fetch peats from the peat-stack, and do all the little odd jobs that nobody else would do.

So poor Assipattle had rather a hard life of it, and he would often have been very miserable had it not been for his sister, who loved him dearly, and who would listen quite patiently to all the stories that he had to tell; who never laughed at him or told him that he was telling lies, as his brothers did.

But one day a very sad thing happened – at least, it was a sad thing for poor Assipattle.

For it chanced that the King of these parts had one only daughter, the Princess Gemdelovely, whom he loved dearly, and to whom he denied nothing. And Princess Gemdelovely was in want of a waiting-maid, and as she had seen Assipattle's sister standing by the garden gate as she was riding by one day, and had taken a fancy to her, she asked her father if she might ask her to come and live at the castle and serve her.

Her father agreed at once, as he always did agree to any of her wishes; and sent a messenger in haste to the farmer's house to ask if his daughter would come to the castle to be the Princess's waiting-maid.

And, of course, the farmer was very pleased at the piece of good fortune which had befallen the girl, and so was her mother, and so were her six brothers, all except poor Assipattle, who looked with wistful eyes after his sister as she rode away, proud of her new clothes and of the slippers which her father had made her out of cowhide, which she was to wear in the Palace when she waited on the Princess, for at home she always ran barefoot.

Time passed, and one day a rider rode in hot haste through the country bearing the most terrible tidings. For the evening before, some fishermen, out in their boats, had caught sight of the Mester Stoorworm, which, as everyone in Orkney knows, was the largest, and the first, and the greatest of all sea serpents. It was that beast which, in the Good Book, is called the Leviathan, and if it had been measured in our day, its tail would have touched Iceland, while its snout rested at John-o'-Groat's Head.

And the fishermen had noticed that this fearsome monster had its head turned towards the mainland, and that it opened its mouth and yawned horribly, as if to show that it was hungry, and that, if it were not fed, it would kill every living thing upon the land, both man and beast, bird and creeping thing.

For it was well known that its breath was so poisonous that it consumed as with a burning fire everything that it lighted on. So that, if it pleased the awful creature to lift its head and put forth its breath, like noxious vapour, over the country, in a few weeks the fair farmland would be turned into a region of desolation.

As you may imagine, everyone was almost paralysed with terror at this awful calamity which threatened them; and the King called a solemn meeting of all his counsellors, and asked them if they could devise any way of warding off the danger.

And for three whole days they sat in Council, these grave, bearded men, and many were the suggestions which were made, and many the words of wisdom which were spoken; but, alas! no one was wise enough to think of a way by which the Mester Stoorworm might be driven back.

At last, at the end of the third day, when everyone had given up hope of finding a remedy, the door of the Council Chamber opened and the Queen appeared.

Now the Queen was the King's second wife, and she was

not a favourite in the Kingdom, for she was a proud, insolent woman, who did not behave kindly to her stepdaughter, the Princess Gemdelovely. She spent much more of her time in the company of a great Sorcerer, whom everyone feared and dreaded, than she did in that of the King, her husband.

So the sober counsellors looked at her disapprovingly as she came boldly into the Council Chamber and stood up beside the King's Chair of State, and, speaking in a loud, clear voice, addressed them thus:

'Ye think that ye are brave men and strong, oh, ye Elders, and fit to be the Protectors of the People. And so it may be, when it is mortals that ye are called on to face. But ye are no match for the foe that now threatens our land. Before him your weapons are but as straw. 'Tis not through strength of arm, but through sorcery, that he will be overcome. So listen to my words, even though they be but those of a woman, and take counsel with the great Sorcerer, from whom nothing is hid, but who knows all the mysteries of the earth, and of the air, and of the sea.'

Now the King and his counsellors did not like this advice, for they hated the Sorcerer, who had, as they thought, too much influence with the Queen; but they were at their wits' end, and knew not to whom to turn for help, so they agreed to do as she said and summon the Wizard before them.

And when he obeyed the summons and appeared in their midst, they liked him none the better for his looks. For he was long, and thin, and awesome, with a beard that came down to his knees, and hair that wrapped him about like a mantle, and his face was the colour of mortar, as if he had always lived in darkness, and had been afraid to look on the sun.

But there was no help to be found in any other man, so they laid the case before him, and asked him what they should do. And he answered coldly that he would think over the matter, and come again to the Assembly the following day and give them his advice.

And his advice, when they heard it, was like to turn their hair white with horror.

For he said that the only way to satisfy the Monster, and to make it spare the land, was to feed it every Saturday with seven young maidens, who must be the fairest who could be found; and if, after this remedy had been tried once or twice, it did not succeed in mollifying the Stoorworm and inducing him to depart, there was but one other measure that he could suggest, but that was so horrible and dreadful that he would not rend their hearts by mentioning it in the meantime.

And as, although they hated him, they feared him also, the Council had to abide by his words, and they pronounced the awful doom.

And so it came about that, every Saturday, seven bonnie, innocent maidens were bound hand and foot and laid on a rock which ran into the sea, and the Monster stretched out his long, jagged tongue, and swept them into his mouth; while all the rest of the folk looked on from the top of a high hill – or, at least, the men looked – with cold, set faces, while the women hid theirs in their aprons and wept aloud.

'Is there no other way,' they cried, 'no other way than this, to save the land?'

But the men only groaned and shook their heads. 'No other way,' they answered; 'no other way.'

Then suddenly a boy's indignant voice rang out among the crowd. 'Is there no grown man who would fight that monster, and kill him, and save the lassies alive? I would do it; I am not feared for the Mester Stoorworm.'

It was the boy Assipattle who spoke, and everyone looked at him in amazement as he stood staring at the great sea serpent, his fingers twitching with rage, and his great blue eyes glowing with pity and indignation.

'The poor bairn's mad; the sight has turned his head,' they whispered one to another; and they would have crowded round him to pet and comfort him, but his elder brother came and gave him a heavy clout on the side of his head.

'*You* fight the Stoorworm!' he cried contemptuously. 'A likely story! Go home to your ash-pit, and stop speaking havers;' and, taking his arm, he drew him to the place where his other brothers were waiting, and they all went home together.

But all the time Assipattle kept on saying that he meant to kill the Stoorworm; and at last his brothers became so angry at what they thought was mere bragging, that they picked up stones and pelted him so hard with them that he took to his heels and ran away from them.

That evening the six brothers were threshing corn in the barn, and Assipattle, as usual, was lying among the ashes thinking his own thoughts, when his mother came out and bade him run and tell the others to come in for their supper.

The boy did as he was bid, for he was a willing enough little fellow; but when he entered the barn his brothers, in revenge for his having run away from them in the afternoon, set on him and pulled him down, and piled so much straw on top of him that, had his father not come from the farmhouse to see what they were all waiting for, he would certainly have been smothered.

But when, at supper-time, his mother was quarrelling with the other lads for what they had done, and saying to them that it was only cowards who set on bairns littler and younger than themselves, Assipattle looked up from the bowl of porridge which he was supping.

'Don't vex yourself, Mother,' he said, 'for I could have fought them all if I liked; ay, and beaten them, too.'

'Why didn't you try it then?' cried everybody at once.

'Because I knew that I would need all my strength when I go to fight the Giant Stoorworm,' replied Assipattle gravely.

111

And, as you may fancy, the others laughed louder than before.

Time passed, and every Saturday seven lassies were thrown to the Stoorworm, until at last it was felt that this state of things could not be allowed to go on any longer; for if it did, there would soon be no maidens at all left in Orkney.

So the Elders met once more, and, after long consultation, it was agreed that the Sorcerer should be summoned, and asked what his other remedy was. 'For, in truth,' said they, 'it cannot be worse than that which we are practising now.'

But, had they known it, the new remedy was even more dreadful than the old. For the cruel Queen hated her step-daughter, Gemdelovely, and the wicked Sorcerer knew that she did, and that she would not be sorry to get rid of her, and, things being as they were, he thought that he saw a way to please the Queen. So he stood up in the Council, and, pretending to be very sorry, said that the only other thing that could be done was to give the Princess Gem-delovely to the Stoorworm, and then it would surely depart.

When they heard this sentence a terrible stillness fell upon the Council, and everyone covered his face with his hands, for no man dare look at the King.

But although his dear daughter was as the apple of his eye, he was a just and righteous monarch, and he felt that it was not right that other fathers should have been forced to part with their daughters, in order to try and save the country, if his child was to be spared.

So, after he had had speech with the Princess, he stood up before the Elders, and declared, with trembling voice, that both he and she were ready to make the sacrifice.

'She is my only child,' he said, 'and the last of her race. Yet it seems good to both of us that she should lay down her life, if by so doing she may save the land that she loves so well.'

Salt tears ran down the faces of the great bearded men as they heard their King's words, for they all knew how dear the Princess Gemdelovely was to him. But it was felt that what he said was wise and true, and that the thing was just and right; for it was better, surely, that one maiden should die, even though she were of royal blood, than that bands of other maidens should go to their death week by week, and all to no purpose.

So, amid heavy sobs, the aged deemster – the lawman who was the chief man of the Council – rose up to pronounce the Princess's doom. But, ere he did so, the King's kemper-man – or fighting-man – stepped forward.

'I ask that this doom should have a tail, just like the Stoorworm! A tail with a sting in it, what's more! If, after devouring our dear Princess the monster has still not de-parted, the next thing that is offered to him will be no tender young maiden, but that tough, lean old Sorcerer.'

And at the kemper-man's words there was such a great shout of approval that the wicked Sorcerer seemed to shrink within himself, and his pale face grew even paler than it was before.

Now, three weeks were allowed between the time that the doom was pronounced upon the Princess and the time that it was carried out, so that the King might send ambassadors to all the neighbouring kingdoms to issue proclamations that, if any champion would come forward who was able to drive away the Stoorworm and save the Princess, he should have her for his wife.

And with her he should have the Kingdom of Orkney, as well as a very famous sword that was now in the King's possession, but which had belonged to the great god Odin, with which he had fought and vanquished all his foes.

The sword bore the name of Sickersnapper, and no man had any power against it.

The news of all these things spread over the length and breadth of the land, and everyone mourned for the fate that was likely to befall the Princess Gemdelovely. And the farmer, and his wife, and their six sons mourned also – all but Assipattle, who sat amongst the ashes and said nothing.

When the King's proclamation was made known throughout the neighbouring kingdoms, there was a fine stir among all the young gallants, for it seemed but a little thing to slay a sea monster; and a beautiful wife, a fertile kingdom, and a trusty sword are not to be won every day.

So six-and-thirty champions arrived at the King's Palace, each hoping to gain the prize.

But the King sent them all out to look at the Giant Stoorworm lying in the sea with its enormous mouth open, and when they saw it, twelve of them were seized with sudden illness, and twelve of them were so afraid that they took to their heels and ran, and never stopped till they reached their own countries; and so only twelve returned to the King's Palace, and as for them, they were so downcast at the thought of the task that they swore had no spirit left in them at all.

And none of them dare try to kill the Stoorworm; so the three weeks passed slowly by, until the night before the day on which the Princess was to be sacrificed. On that night the King, feeling that he must do something to entertain his guests, made a great supper for them.

But, as you may guess, it was a dreary feast, for everyone was thinking so much about the terrible thing that was to happen on the morrow, that no one could eat or drink.

And when it was all over, and everybody had retired to rest, save the King and his old kemper-man, the King returned to the great hall, and went slowly up to his Chair of State, high up on the dais. It was not like the Chairs of State that we know nowadays; it was nothing but a massive kist, in which he kept all the things which he treasured most.

The old monarch undid the iron bolts with trembling fingers, and lifted the lid, and took out the wondrous sword, Sickersnapper, which had belonged to the great god Odin.

His trusty kemper-man, who had stood by him in a hundred fights, watched him with pitying eyes.

'Why lift out the sword,' he said softly, 'when your fighting days are done? Right nobly have you fought your battles in the past, oh, my Lord! when your arm was strong and sure. But when folk's years number four score and sixteen, as yours do, 'tis time to leave such work to other and younger men.'

The old King turned on him angrily, with something of the old fire in his eyes. 'Wheesht,' he cried, 'else will I turn this sword on you. Do you think that I can see my only bairn devoured by a monster, and not lift a finger to try and save her when no other man will? I tell you – and I will swear it with my two thumbs crossed on Sickersnapper – that both the sword and I will be destroyed before so much as one of her hairs be touched. So go, if you love me, my old comrade, and order my boat to be ready, with the sail set and the prow pointed out to sea. I will go myself and fight the Stoorworm; and if I do not return, I will lay it on you to guard my cherished daughter. Peradventure, my life may redeem hers.'

Now that night everybody at the farm went to bed early, for next morning the whole family was to set out first thing, to go to the top of the hill near the sea, to see the Princess eaten by the Stoorworm. All except Assipattle, who was to be left at home to herd the geese.

The lad was so vexed at this – for he had great schemes in his head – that he could not sleep. And as he lay tossing and tumbling about in his corner among the ashes, he heard his father and mother talking in the great box-bed. And, as he listened, he found that they were having an argument.

''Tis such a long way to the hill overlooking the sea, I fear me I shall never walk it,' said his mother. 'I think I had better bide at home.'

'Nay,' replied her husband, 'that would be a bonny-like

thing, when all the countryside is to be there. You will ride behind me on my good mare Go-swift.'

'I do not care to trouble you to take me behind you,' said his wife, 'for I think you don't love me as you used to do.'

'The woman's havering,' cried the Goodman of the house impatiently. 'What makes you think that I have ceased to love you?'

'Because you no longer tell me your secrets,' answered his wife. 'To go no further, think of this very horse, Go-swift. For five long years I have been begging you to tell me how it is that, when *you* ride her, she flies faster than the wind, while if any other man mount her, she hirples along like a broken-down nag.'

The Goodman laughed. ''Twas not for lack of love for you that I kept that a secret, Goodwife,' he said, 'though it might be for lack of trust. For women's tongues wag but loosely; and I did not want other folk to ken my secret. But since my silence has vexed your heart, I'll tell you everything.

'When I want Go-swift to stand, I give her one clap on the left shoulder. When I would have her go like any other horse, I give her two claps on the right. But when I want her to fly like the wind, I whistle through the windpipe of a goose. And, as I never ken when I want her to gallop like that, I aye keep the bird's thrapple in the left-hand pocket of my coat.'

'So *that* is how you manage the beast,' said the farmer's wife, in a satisfied tone; 'and that is what becomes of all my goose thrapples. Oh! but you're a clever fellow, Goodman; and now that I ken the way of it I may go to sleep.'

Assipattle was not tumbling about in the ashes now; he was sitting up in the darkness, with glowing cheeks and sparkling eyes.

His opportunity had come at last, and he knew it.

He waited patiently till their heavy breathing told him

that his parents were asleep; then he crept over to where his father's clothes were, and took the goose's windpipe out of the pocket of his coat, and slipped noiselessly out of the house. Once he was out of it, he ran like lightning to the stable. He saddled and bridled Go-swift, and threw a halter round her neck, and led her to the stable door.

The good mare, unaccustomed to her new groom, pranced, and reared, and plunged; but Assipattle, knowing his father's secret, clapped her once on the left shoulder, and she stood as still as a stone. Then he mounted her, and gave her two claps on the right shoulder, and the good horse trotted off briskly, giving a loud neigh as she did so.

The unwonted sound, ringing out in the stillness of the night, roused the household, and the Goodman and his six sons came tumbling down the wooden stairs, shouting to one another in confusion that someone was stealing Go-swift.

The farmer was the first to reach the door; and when he saw, in the starlight, the vanishing form of his favourite steed, he cried at the top of his voice:

> 'Stop thief, ho!
> Go-swift, whoa!'

And when Go-swift heard that she pulled up in a moment. All seemed lost, for the farmer and his sons could run very fast indeed, and it seemed to Assipattle, sitting motionless on Go-swift's back, that they would very soon make up on him.

But, luckily, he remembered the goose's thrapple, and he pulled it out of his pocket and whistled through it. In an instant the good mare bounded forward, swift as the wind, and was over the hill and out of sight of its pursuers before they had taken ten steps more.

Day was dawning when the lad came within view of the

sea; and there, in front of him, in the water, lay the enormous monster whom he had come so far to slay. Anyone would have said that he was mad even to dream of making such an attempt, for he was but a slim, unarmed youth, and the Mester Stoorworm was so big that men said it would reach the fourth part round the world. And its tongue was jagged at the end like a fork, and with this fork it could sweep whatever it chose into its mouth, and devour it at its leisure.

For all this, Assipattle was not afraid, for he had the heart of a hero underneath his tattered garments. 'I must be cautious,' he said to himself, 'and do by my wits what I cannot do by my strength.'

He climbed down from his seat on Go-swift's back, and tethered the good steed to a tree, and walked on, looking well about him, till he came to a little cottage on the edge of a little wood.

The door was not locked, so he entered, and found its occupant, an old woman, fast asleep in bed. He did not disturb her, but he took down an iron pot from the shelf, and examined it closely.

'This will serve my purpose,' he said; 'and surely the old dame would not grudge it if she knew it was to save the Princess's life.'

Then he lifted a live peat from the smouldering fire, and went his way.

Down at the water's edge he found the King's boat lying, guarded by a single boatman, with its sails set and its prow turned in the direction of the Mester Stoorworm.

'It's a cold morning,' said Assipattle. 'Are you not well-nigh frozen sitting there? If you'll come ashore, and run about, and warm yourself, I will get into the boat and guard it till you return.'

'A likely story,' replied the man. 'And what would the King say if he were to come, as I expect every moment he will do, and find me playing myself on the sand, and his good boat left to a wee laddie like you? 'Twould be as much as my head is worth.'

'As you will,' answered Assipattle carelessly, beginning to search among the rocks. 'In the mean time, I must be looking for a few mussels to roast for my breakfast.' And after he had gathered the mussels, he began to make a hole in the sand to put the live peat in. The boatman watched him curiously, for he, too, was beginning to feel hungry.

Presently the lad gave a wild shriek, and jumped high in the air. 'Gold, gold!' he cried. 'By the name of Thor, who would have looked to find gold here?'

This was too much for the boatman. Forgetting all about his head and the King, he jumped out of the boat, and, pushing Assipattle aside, began to scrape among the sand with all his might.

While he was doing so, Assipattle seized his pot, jumped into the boat, and pushed off. He was half a mile out to sea before the outwitted man, who, needless to say, could find no gold, noticed what he was about.

And, of course, he was very angry, and the old King was more angry still when he came down to the shore, attended by his nobles and carrying the great sword Sickersnapper, in the vain hope that he, poor feeble old man that he was, might be able in some way to defeat the monster and save his daughter.

But to make such an attempt was beyond his power now that his boat was gone. So he could only stand on the shore, along with the fast assembling crowd of his subjects, and watch what would befall.

And this was what befell.

Assipattle, sailing slowly over the sea, and watching the Mester Stoorworm intently, noticed that the terrible monster yawned occasionally, as if longing for his weekly feast. And as it yawned a great flood of sea-water went down its throat, and came out again at its huge gills.

119

So the brave lad took down his sail, and pointed the prow of his boat straight at the monster's mouth, and the next time it yawned he and his boat were sucked right in, and, like Jonah, went straight down its throat into the dark regions inside its body. On and on the boat floated; but as it went the water grew less, pouring out of the Stoorworm's gills, till at last it stuck, as it were, on dry land. And Assipattle jumped out, his pot in his hand, and began to explore.

Presently he came to the huge creature's liver, and, having heard that the liver of a fish is full of oil, he made a hole in it and put in the live peat.

Woe's me! but there was a conflagration! And Assipattle just got back to his boat in time; for the Mester Stoorworm, in its convulsions, threw the boat right out of its mouth again, and it was flung up, high and dry, on the bare land.

The commotion in the sea was so terrible that the King and his daughter – who by this time had come down to the shore dressed like a bride, in white, ready to be thrown to the monster – and all his courtiers, and all the country-folk, were fain to take refuge on the hilltop, out of harm's way, and stand and see what happened next.

And this was what happened next.

The poor, distressed creature – for it was now to be pitied, even although it was a great, cruel, awful Mester Stoorworm – tossed itself to and fro, twisting and writhing.

And as it tossed its awful head out of the water its tongue fell out, and struck the earth with such force that it made a great dent in it, into which the sea rushed. And that dent formed the crooked Straits which now divide Denmark from Norway and Sweden.

Then some of its teeth fell out and rested in the sea, and became the islands that we now call the Shetland Isles; and a little afterwards some more teeth dropped out, and they became what we now call the Faeroe Isles.

After that the creature twisted itself into a great lump and died; and this lump became the island of Iceland; and the fire which Assipattle had kindled with his live peat still burns on underneath it, and that is why there are mountains which throw out fire in that chilly land.

When at last it was plainly seen that the Mester Stoorworm was dead, the King could scarce contain himself with joy. He put his arms round Assipattle's neck, and kissed him, and called him his son. And he took off his own royal mantle and put it on the lad, and girded his good sword Sickersnapper round his waist. And he called his daughter, the Princess Gemdelovely, to him, and put her hand in his, and declared that when the right time came she should be his wife, and that he should be ruler over all the Kingdom of Orkney.

Then the whole company mounted their horses again, and Assipattle rode on Go-swift by the Princess's side; and so they returned, with great joy, to the King's Palace.

But as they were nearing the gate Assipattle's sister, she who was the Princess's maid, ran out to meet him, and signed to the Princess to lean down, and whispered something in her ear.

The Princess's face grew dark, and she turned her horse's head and rode back to where her father was, with his nobles. She told him the words that the maiden had spoken; and when he heard them his face, too, grew as black as thunder.

For the matter was this: the cruel Queen, full of joy at the thought that she was to be rid, once and for all, of her stepdaughter, had been making love to the wicked Sorcerer all the morning in the old King's absence.

'He shall be killed at once,' cried the monarch. 'Such behaviour cannot be overlooked.'

'You will have much ado to find him, your Majesty,' said the girl, 'for more than an hour since he and the Queen fled together on the fleetest horses that they could find in the stables.'

'But I can find him,' cried Assipattle; and he went off like the wind on his good horse Go-swift.

It was not long before he came within sight of the fugitives, and he drew his sword and shouted to them to stop.

They heard the shout and turned round, and they both laughed aloud in derision when they saw that it was only the boy who grovelled in the ashes who pursued them.

'The insolent brat! I will cut off his head for him! I will teach him a lesson!' cried the Sorcerer; and he rode boldly back to meet Assipattle. For although he was no fighter, he knew that no ordinary weapon could harm his enchanted body; therefore he was not afraid.

But he did not count on Assipattle having the sword of the great god Odin, with which he had slain all his enemies; and before this magic weapon the Sorcerer was powerless. And, at one thrust, the young lad ran it through his body as easily as if he had been any ordinary man, and he fell from his horse, dead.

Then the courtiers of the King, who had also set off in pursuit, but whose steeds were less fleet of foot than Go-swift, came up, and seized the bridle of the Queen's horse, and led it and its rider back to the Palace.

She was brought before the Council, and judged, and condemned to be shut up in a high tower for the remainder of her life. Which thing surely came to pass.

As for Assipattle, when the proper time came he was married to the Princess Gemdelovely, with great feasting and rejoicing. And when the old King died they ruled the kingdom for many a long year.

Part Three

APPARITIONS,
SECOND SIGHT AND
WITCHES

ADAM BELL

James Hogg

This tale, which may be depended on as in every part true, is singular, from the circumstance of its being insolvable, either from the facts that have been discovered relating to it, or by reason; for though events sometimes occur among mankind, which at the time seem inexplicable, yet there are always some individuals acquainted with the primary causes of these events, and they seldom fail of being brought to light before all the actors in them, or their confidants, are removed from this state of existence. But the causes which produced the events here related have never been accounted for in this world; even conjecture is left to wander in a labyrinth, unable to get hold of the thread that leads to the catastrophe.

Mr Bell was a gentleman of Annandale, in Dumfriesshire, in the south of Scotland, and proprietor of a considerable estate in that district, part of which he occupied himself. He lost his father when he was an infant, and his mother, dying when he was about twenty years of age, left him the sole proprietor of the estate, besides a large sum of money at interest, for which he was indebted, in a great measure, to his mother's parsimony during his minority. His person was tall, comely, and athletic, and his whole delight was in warlike and violent exercises. He was the best horseman and marksman in the county, and valued himself particularly upon his skill in the broadsword. Of this he often boasted aloud, and regretted that there was not one in the county whose skill was in some degree equal to his own.

In the autumn of 1745, after being for several days busily and silently employed in preparing for his journey, he left his own house, and went to Edinburgh, giving at the same time such directions to his servants as indicated his intention of being absent for some time.

A few days after he had left his home, one morning, while his housekeeper was putting the house in order for the day, her master, as she thought, entered by the kitchen door, the other being bolted, and passed her in the middle of the floor. He was buttoned in his greatcoat, which was the same he had on when he went from home; he likewise had the same hat on his head, and the same whip in his hand which he took with him. At sight of him she uttered a shriek, but recovering her surprise, instantly said to him, 'You have not stayed so long from us, Sir.' He made no reply, but went sullenly into his own room, without throwing off his greatcoat. After a pause of about five minutes, she followed him into the room. He was standing at his desk with his back towards her. She asked him if he wished to have a fire kindled, and afterwards if he was well enough; but he still made no reply to any of these questions. She was astonished, and returned into the kitchen. After tarrying about another five minutes, he went out at the front door, it being then open, and walked deliberately towards the bank of the River Kinnel, which was deep and wooded, and in that he vanished from her sight. The woman ran out in the utmost consternation to acquaint the men who were servants belonging to the house; and coming to one of the ploughmen, she told him that their master was come home, and had certainly lost his reason, for he was wandering about the house and would not speak. The man loosed his horses from the plough and came home, listened to the woman's story, made her repeat it again and again, and then assured her that she was raving, for their master's horse was not in the stable, and of course he could not be come home. However, as she persisted in her claim, with every appearance of sincerity, he went down to the river to see what was become of his mysterious master. He was neither to be seen nor heard of in all the country. It was then concluded that the housekeeper had seen an apparition, and that something had befallen their master; but on consulting with some old people, skilled in these matters, they learned that when a 'wraith', or apparition of a living person, appeared while the sun was up, instead of being a prelude of instant death, it prognosticated very long life; and, moreover, that it could not possibly be a ghost that she had seen, for they always chose the night season for making their visits. In short, though it was the general topic of conversation among the servants and the people in the vicinity, no reasonable conclusion could be formed on the subject.

The most probable conjecture was that as Mr Bell was known to be so fond of arms, and had left his home on the very day that Prince Charles Stuart and his Highlanders defeated General Hawley on Falkirk Muir, he had gone either with him or the Duke of Cumberland to the north. It was, however, afterwards ascertained that he had never joined any of the armies. Week passed after week, and month after month, but no word of Mr Bell. A female cousin was his nearest living relation; her husband took the management of his affairs; and concluding that he had either joined the army, or drowned himself in the Kinnel, when he was seen going down to the river, made no more inquiries after him.

About this very time, a respectable farmer, whose surname was McMillan, and who resided in the neighbourhood of Musselburgh, happened to be in Edinburgh about some business. In the evening he called upon a friend who lived near Holyrood House; and being seized with an indisposition, they persuaded him to tarry with them all night. About the middle of the night he grew exceedingly ill, and, not being able to find any rest or ease in his bed, imagined he would be the better of a walk. He put on his clothes, and, that he might not disturb the family, slipped quietly out at the back door, and walked in St Anthony's garden behind the house. The moon shone so bright, that it was almost as light as noonday, and he had scarcely taken a single turn, when he saw a tall man enter from the other side, buttoned in a drab-coloured greatcoat. It so happened that at that time McMillan stood in the shadow of the wall, and perceiving that the stranger did not observe him, a thought struck him that it would not be amiss to keep himself concealed, that he might see what the man was going to be about. The man walked backwards and forwards for some time in apparent impatience, looking at his watch every minute, until at length another man came in by the same way, buttoned likewise in a greatcoat, and having a bonnet on his head. He was remarkably stout made, but considerably lower in stature than the other. They exchanged only a single word; then turning both about, they threw off their coats, drew their swords, and began a most desperate and well-contested combat.

The tall gentleman appeared to have the advantage. He constantly gained ground on the other, and drove him half round the division of the garden in which they fought. Each of them strove to fight with his back towards the moon, so that it might shine full in the face of his opponent; and many rapid wheels were made for the purpose of gaining this position. The engagement was long and obstinate, and by the desperate thrusts that were frequently aimed on both sides, it was evident that they meant one another's destruction. They came at length within a few yards of the place where McMillan still stood concealed. They were both out of breath, and at that instant a small cloud chancing to overshadow the moon, one of them called out, 'Hold, we cannot see.' They uncovered their heads, wiped their faces, and as soon as the moon emerged from the cloud, each resumed his guard. Surely that was an awful pause! And short, indeed, was the stage between it and eternity with the one! The tall gentleman made a lunge at the other, who parried and returned it; and as the former sprung back to avoid the thrust, his foot slipped, and he stumbled forward towards his antagonist, who dextrously met his breast in the fall with the point of his sword, and ran him through the body. He made only one feeble convulsive struggle, as if attempting to rise, and expired almost instantaneously.

McMillan was petrified with horror; but conceiving himself to be in a perilous situation, having stolen out of the house at that dead hour of the night, he had so much presence of mind as to hold his peace, and to keep from interfering in the smallest degree.

The surviving combatant wiped his sword with great composure, put on his bonnet, covered the body with one of the greatcoats, took up the other, and departed. McMillan returned quietly to his chamber without awakening any of the family. His pains were gone, but his mind was shocked and exceedingly perturbed; and after deliberating until morning, he determined to say nothing of the matter, and to make no living creature acquainted with what he had seen, thinking that suspicion would infallibly rest on him. Accordingly, he kept his bed next morning, until his friend brought him the tidings that a gentleman had been murdered at the back of the house during the night. He then arose and examined the body, which was that of a young man, seemingly from the country, having brown hair, and fine manly features. He had neither letter, book, nor signature of any kind about him that could in the least lead to a discovery of who he was; only a common silver watch was found in his pocket, and an elegant sword was clasped in his cold bloody hand, which had an A and B engraved on the hilt. The sword had entered at his breast, and gone out at his back a little below the left shoulder. He had likewise received a slight wound on the sword arm.

The body was carried to the mortuary, where it lay for eight days, and though great numbers inspected it, yet none knew who or whence the deceased was, and he was at length buried among the strangers in Greyfriars churchyard.

Sixteen years elapsed before McMillan mentioned to any person the circumstance of his having seen the duel, but at that period, being in Annandale receiving some sheep that he had bought, and chancing to hear of the astonishing circumstances of Bell's disappearance, he divulged the whole. The time, the description of his person, his clothes, and, above all, the sword with the initials of his name engraved upon it, confirmed the fact beyond the smallest shadow of doubt that it was Mr Bell whom he had seen killed in the duel behind the abbey. But who the person was that slew him, how the quarrel commenced, or who it was that appeared to his housekeeper, remains to this day a profound secret, and is likely to remain so, until that day when every deed of darkness shall be brought to light.

Some have even ventured to blame McMillan for the whole, on account of his long concealment of facts, and likewise in consideration of his uncommon bodily strength and daring disposition, he being one of the boldest and most enterprising men of the age in which he lived; but all who knew him despised such insinuations, and declared them to be entirely inconsistent with his character, which was most honourable and disinterested; and besides, his tale has every appearance of truth.

THE GREY WOLF

George MacDonald

One evening-twilight in spring, a young English student, who had wandered northwards as far as the outlying fragments of Scotland called the Orkney and Shetland Islands, found himself on a small island of the latter group, caught in a storm of wind and hail, which had come on suddenly. It was in vain to look about for any shelter; for not only did the storm entirely obscure the landscape, but there was nothing around him save a desert moss.

At length, however, as he walked on for mere walking's sake, he found himself on the verge of a cliff, and saw, over the brow of it, a few feet below him, a ledge of rock, where he might find some shelter from the blast, which blew from behind. Letting himself down by his hands, he alighted upon something that crunched beneath his tread, and found the bones of many small animals scattered about in front of a little cave in the rock, offering the refuge he sought. He went in, and sat upon a stone. The storm increased in violence, and as the darkness grew he became uneasy, for he

did not relish the thought of spending the night in the cave. He had parted from his companions on the opposite side of the island, and it added to his uneasiness that they must be full of apprehension about him. At last there came a lull in the storm, and the same instant he heard a footfall, stealthy and light as that of a wild beast, upon the bones at the mouth of the cave. He started up in some fear, though the least thought might have satisfied him that there could be no very dangerous animals upon the island. Before he had time to think, however, the face of a woman appeared in the opening. Eagerly the wanderer spoke. She started at the sound of his voice. He could not see her well, because she was turned towards the darkness of the cave.

'Will you tell me how to find my way across the moor to Shielness?' he asked.

'You cannot find it tonight,' she answered, in a sweet tone, and with a smile that bewitched him, revealing the whitest of teeth.

'What am I to do, then?' he asked.

'My mother will give you shelter, but that is all she has to offer.'

'And that is far more than I expected a minute ago,' he replied. 'I shall be most grateful.'

She turned in silence and left the cave. The youth followed.

She was barefooted, and her pretty brown feet went catlike over the sharp stones, as she led the way down a rocky path to the shore. Her garments were scanty and torn, and her hair blew tangled in the wind. She seemed about five and twenty, lithe and small. Her long fingers kept clutching and pulling nervously at her skirts as she went. Her face was very grey in complexion, and very worn, but delicately formed, and smooth-skinned. Her thin nostrils were tremulous as eyelids, and her lips, whose curves were faultless, had no colour to give sign of indwelling blood. What her eyes were like he could not see, for she had never lifted the delicate films of her eyelids.

At the foot of the cliff they came upon a little hut leaning against it, and having for its inner apartment a natural hollow within it. Smoke was spreading over the face of the rock, and the grateful odour of food gave hope to the hungry student. His guide opened the door of the cottage; he followed her in, and saw a woman bending over a fire in the middle of the floor. On the fire lay a large fish broiling. The daughter spoke a few words, and the mother turned and welcomed the stranger. She had an old and very wrinkled, but honest face, and looked troubled. She dusted the only chair in the cottage, and placed it for him by the side of the fire, opposite the one window, whence he saw a little patch of yellow sand over which the spent waves spread themselves out listlessly. Under this window there was a bench, upon which the daughter threw herself in an unusual posture, resting her chin upon her hand. A moment after the youth caught the first glimpse of her blue eyes. They were fixed upon him with a strange look of greed, amounting to craving, but as if aware that they belied or betrayed her, she dropped them instantly. The moment she veiled them, her face, notwithstanding its colourless complexion, was almost beautiful.

When the fish was ready, the old woman wiped the deal table, steadied it upon the uneven floor, and covered it with a piece of fine table-linen. She then laid the fish on a wooden platter, and invited the guest to help himself. Seeing no other provision, he pulled from his pocket a hunting knife, and divided a portion from the fish, offering it to the mother first.

'Come, my lamb,' said the old woman; and the daughter approached the table. But her nostrils and mouth quivered with disgust.

The next moment she turned and hurried from the hut.

'She doesn't like fish,' said the old woman, 'and I haven't anything else to give her.'

'She does not seem in good health,' he rejoined.

The woman answered only with a sigh, and they ate their fish with the help of a little rye-bread. As they finished their supper, the youth heard a sound like the pattering of a dog's feet upon the sand close to the door; but ere he had time to look out of the window, the door opened and the young woman entered. She looked better, perhaps from having just washed her face. She drew a stool to the corner of the fire opposite him. But as she sat down, to his bewilderment, and even horror, the student spied a single drop of blood on her white skin within her torn dress. The woman brought out a jar of whisky, put a rusty old kettle on the fire, and took her place in front of it. As soon as the water boiled, she proceeded to make some toddy in a wooden bowl.

Meantime the youth could not take his eyes off the young

woman, so that at length he found himself fascinated, or rather bewitched. She kept her eyes for the most part veiled with the loveliest eyelids fringed with darkest lashes, and he gazed entranced; for the red glow of the little oil-lamp covered all the strangeness of her complexion. But as soon as he met a stolen glance out of those eyes unveiled, his soul shuddered within him. Lovely face and craving eyes alternated fascination and repulsion.

The mother placed the bowl in his hands. He drank sparingly, and passed it to the girl. She lifted it to her lips, and as she tasted – only tasted it – looked at him. He thought the drink must have been drugged and have affected his brain. Her hair smoothed itself back, and drew her forehead backwards with it; while the lower part of her face projected towards the bowl, revealing, ere she sipped, her dazzling teeth in strange prominence. But the same moment the vision vanished; she returned the vessel to her mother and, rising, hurried out of the cottage.

Then the old woman pointed to a bed of heather in one corner with a murmured apology; and the student, wearied both with the fatigues of the day and the strangeness of the night, threw himself upon it, wrapped in his cloak. The moment he lay down, the storm began afresh, and the wind blew so keenly through the crannies of the hut, that it was only by drawing his cloak over his head that he could protect himself from its currents. Unable to sleep, he lay listening to the uproar which grew in violence, till the spray was dashing against the window. At length the door opened, and the young woman came in, made up the fire, drew the bench before it, and lay down in the same strange posture, with her chin propped on her hand and elbow, and her face turned towards the youth. He moved a little; she dropped her head, and lay on her face, with her arms crossed beneath her forehead. The mother had disappeared.

Drowsiness crept over him. A movement of the bench

roused him, and he fancied he saw some four-footed creature as tall as a large dog trot quietly out of the door. He was sure he felt a rush of cold wind. Gazing fixedly through the darkness, he thought he saw the eyes of the damsel encountering his, but a glow from the falling together of the remnants of the fire, revealed clearly enough that the bench was vacant. Wondering what could have made her go out in such a storm, he fell fast asleep.

In the middle of the night he felt a pain in his shoulder, came broad awake, and saw the gleaming eyes and grinning teeth of some animal close to his face. Its claws were in his shoulder, and its mouth in the act of seeking his throat. Before it had fixed its fangs, however, he had its throat in one hand, and sought his knife with the other. A terrible struggle followed; but regardless of the tearing claws, he found and opened his knife. He had made one futile stab, and was drawing it for a surer, when, with a spring of the whole body, and one wildly-contorted effort, the creature twisted its neck from his hold, and with something betwixt a scream and a howl, darted from him. Again he heard the door open; again the wind blew in upon him, and it continued blowing; a sheet of spray dashed across the floor, and over his face. He sprung from his couch and bounded to the door.

It was a wild night – dark, but for the flash of whiteness from the waves as they broke within a few yards of the cottage; the wind was raving, and the rain pouring down the air. A gruesome sound as of mingled weeping and howling came from somewhere in the dark. He turned again into the hut and closed the door, but could find no way of securing it.

The lamp was nearly out, and he could not be certain whether the form of the young woman was upon the bench or not. Overcoming a strong repugnance, he approached it, and put out his hands – there was nothing there. He sat down and waited for the daylight: he dared not sleep any more.

When the day dawned at length, he went out yet again, and looked around. The morning was dim and gusty and grey. The wind had fallen, but the waves were tossing wildly. He wandered up and down the little strand, longing for more light.

At length he heard a movement in the cottage. By and by the voice of the old woman called to him from the door.

'You're up early, sir. I suppose you didn't sleep well.'

'Not very well,' he answered. 'But where is your daughter?'

'She's not awake yet,' said the mother. 'I'm afraid I have but a poor breakfast for you. But you'll take a dram and a bit of fish. It's all I've got.'

Unwilling to hurt her, though hardly in good appetite, he sat down at the table. While they were eating, the daughter came in, but turned her face away and went to the further end of the hut. When she came forward after a minute or two, the youth saw that her hair was drenched, and her face whiter than before. She looked ill and faint, and when she raised her eyes, all their fierceness had vanished, and sadness had taken its place. Her neck was now covered with a cotton handkerchief. She was modestly attentive to him, and no longer shunned his gaze. He was gradually yielding to the temptation of braving another night in the hut, and seeing what would follow, when the old woman spoke.

'The weather will be broken all day, sir,' she said. 'You had better be going, or your friends will leave without you.'

Ere he could answer, he saw such a beseeching glance on the face of the girl, that he hesitated, confused. Glancing at the mother, he saw the flash of wrath in her face. She rose and approached her daughter, with her hand lifted to strike her. The young woman stooped her head with a cry. He darted round the table to interpose between them. But the mother had caught hold of her; the handkerchief had fallen from her neck; and the youth saw five blue bruises on her lovely throat – the marks of the four fingers and the thumb of a left hand. With a cry of horror he darted from the house, but as he reached the door he turned. His hostess was lying motionless on the floor, and a huge grey wolf came bounding after him.

There was no weapon at hand; and if there had been, his inborn chivalry would never have allowed him to harm a woman even under the guise of a wolf. Instinctively, he set himself firm, leaning a little forward, with half outstretched arms, and hands curved ready to clutch again at the throat upon which he had left those pitiful marks. But the creature as she sprung eluded his grasp, and just as he expected to feel her fangs, he found a woman weeping on his bosom, with her arms around his neck. The next instant, the grey wolf broke from him, and bounded howling up the cliff. Recovering himself as he best might, the youth followed, for it was the only way to the moor above, across which he must now make his way to find his companions.

All at once he heard the sound of a crunching of bones – not as if a creature was eating them, but as if they were ground by the teeth of rage and disappointment: looking up, he saw close above him the mouth of the little cavern in which he had taken refuge the day before. Summoning all his resolution, he passed it slowly and softly. From within came the sounds of a mingled moaning and growling.

Having reached the top, he ran at full speed for some distance across the moor before venturing to look behind him. When at length he did so, he saw, against the sky, the girl standing on the edge of the cliff, wringing her hands. One solitary wail crossed the space between. She made no attempt to follow him, and he reached the opposite shore in safety.

THROUGH THE VEIL

Sir Arthur Conan Doyle

He was a great shock-headed, freckle-faced Borderer, the lineal descendant of a cattle-thieving clan in Liddesdale. In spite of his ancestry he was as solid and sober a citizen as one would wish to see, a town councillor of Melrose, an elder of the Church, and the chairman of the local branch of the Young Men's Christian Association. Brown was his name – and you saw it printed up as 'Brown and Handiside' over the great grocery stores in the High Street. His wife, Maggie Brown, was an Armstrong before her marriage, and came from an old farming stock in the wilds of Teviothead. She was small, swarthy, and dark-eyed, with a strangely nervous temperament for a Scotswoman. No greater contrast could be found than the big tawny man and the dark little woman, but both were of the soil as far back as any memory could extend.

One day – it was the first anniversary of their wedding – they had driven over together to see the excavations of the Roman fort at Newstead. It was not a particularly picturesque spot. From the northern bank of the Tweed, just where the river forms a loop, there extends a gentle slope of arable land. Across it run the trenches of the excavators, with here and there an exposure of old stonework to show the foundations of the ancient walls. It had been a huge place, for the camp was fifty acres in extent, and the fort fifteen. However, it was all made easy for them since Mr Brown knew the farmer to whom the land belonged. Under his guidance they spent a long summer evening inspecting the trenches, the pits, the ramparts, and all the strange variety of objects which were waiting to be transported to the Edinburgh Museum of Antiquities. The buckle of a woman's belt had been dug up that very day, and the farmer was discoursing upon it when his eyes fell upon Mrs Brown's face.

'Your good leddy's tired,' said he. 'Maybe you'd best rest a wee before we gang further.'

Brown looked at his wife. She was certainly very pale, and her dark eyes were bright and wild.

'What is it, Maggie? I've wearied you. I'm thinkin' it's time we went back.'

'No, no, John, let us go on. It's wonderful! It's like a dreamland place. It all seems so close and so near to me. How long were the Romans here, Mr Cunningham?'

'A fair time, mam. If you saw the kitchen midden-pits you would guess it took a long time to fill them.'

'And why did they leave?'

'Well, mam, by all accounts they left because they had to. The folk round could thole them no longer, so they just up and burned the fort aboot their lugs. You can see the fire marks on the stanes.'

The woman gave a quick little shudder. 'A wild night – a fearsome night,' said she. 'The sky must have been red that night – and these grey stones, they may have been red also.'

'Aye, I think they were red,' said her husband. 'It's a queer thing, Maggie, and it may be your words that have done it; but I seem to see that business aboot as clear as ever I saw anything in my life. The light shone on the water.'

'Aye, the light shone on the water. And the smoke gripped you by the throat. And all the savages were yelling.'

The old farmer began to laugh. 'The leddy will be writin' a story aboot the old fort,' said he. 'I've shown many a one ower it, but I never heard it put so clear afore. Some folk have the gift.'

They had strolled along the edge of the foss, and a pit yawned upon the right of them.

'That pit was fourteen foot deep,' said the farmer. 'What d'ye think we dug oot from the bottom o't? Weel, it was just the skeleton of a man wi' a spear by his side. I'm thinkin' he was grippin' it when he died. Now, how cam' a man wi' a spear doon a hole fourteen foot deep? He wasna' buried there, for they aye burned their dead. What make ye o' that, mam?'

'He sprang doon to get clear of the savages,' said the woman.

'Weel, it's likely enough, and a' the professors from Edinburgh couldna gie a better reason. I wish you were aye here, mam, to answer a' oor deeficulties sae readily. Now, here's the altar that we foond last week. There's an inscreeption. They tell me it's Latin, and it means that the men o' this fort give thanks to God for their safety.'

They examined the old worn stone. There was a large deeply-cut 'VV' upon the top of it.

'What does "VV" stand for?' asked Brown.

'Naebody kens,' the guide answered.

'*Valeria Victrix*,' said the lady softly. Her face was paler than ever, her eyes far away, as one who peers down the dim aisles of over-arching centuries.

'What's that?' asked her husband sharply.

She started as one who wakes from sleep. 'What were we talking about?' she asked.

'About this "VV" upon the stone.'

'No doubt it was just the name of the Legion which put the altar up.'

'Aye, but you gave some special name.'

'Did I? How absurd! How should I ken what the name was?'

'You said something – "*Victrix*", I think.'

'I suppose I was guessing. It gives me the queerest feeling, this place, as if I were not myself, but someone else.'

'Aye, it's an uncanny place,' said her husband, looking round with an expression almost of fear in his bold grey eyes. 'I feel it mysel'. I think we'll just be wishin' you good evenin', Mr Cunningham, and get back to Melrose before the dark sets in.'

Neither of them could shake off the strange impression which had been left upon them by their visit to the excavations. It was as if some miasma had risen from those damp trenches and passed into their blood. All the evening they were silent and thoughtful, but such remarks as they did make showed that the same subject was in the minds of each. Brown had a restless night, in which he dreamed a strange connected dream, so vivid that he woke sweating and shivering like a frightened horse. He tried to convey it all to his wife as they sat together at breakfast in the morning.

'It was the clearest thing, Maggie,' said he. 'Nothing that has ever come to me in my waking life has been more clear than that. I feel as if these hands were sticky with blood.'

'Tell me of it – tell me slow,' said she.

'When it began, I was oot on a braeside. I was laying flat on the ground. It was rough, and there were clumps of heather. All round me was just darkness, but I could hear the rustle and the breathin' of men. There seemed a great multitude on every side of me, but I could see no one. There was a low chink of steel sometimes, and then a number of

143

voices would whisper, "Hush!" I had a ragged club in my hand, and it had spikes o' iron near the end of it. My heart was beatin' quickly, and I felt that a moment of great danger and excitement was at hand. Once I dropped my club, and again from all round me the voices in the darkness cried, "Hush!" I put oot my hand, and it touched the foot of another man lying in front of me. There was someone at my very elbow on either side. But they said nothin'.

'Then we all began to move. The whole braeside seemed to be crawlin' downwards. There was a river at the bottom and a high-arched wooden bridge. Beyond the bridge were many lights – torches on a wall. The creepin' men all flowed towards the bridge. There had been no sound of any kind, just a velvet stillness. And then there was a cry in the darkness, the cry of a man who has been stabbed suddenly to the hairt. That one cry swelled out for a moment, and then the roar of a thoosand furious voices. I was runnin'. Everyone was runnin'. A bright red light shone out, and the river was a scarlet streak. I could see my companions now. They were more like devils than men, wild figures clad in skins, with their hair and beards streamin'. They were all mad with rage, jumpin' as they ran, their mouths open, their arms wavin', the red light beatin' on their faces. I ran, too, and yelled out curses like the rest. Then I heard a great cracklin' of wood, and I knew that the palisades were doon. There was a loud whistlin' in my ears, and I was aware that arrows were flyin' past me. I got to the bottom of a dyke, and I saw a hand stretched doon from above. I took it, and was dragged to the top. We looked doon, and there were silver men beneath us holdin' up their spears. Some of our folk sprang on to the spears. Then we others followed, and we killed the soldiers before they could draw the spears oot again. They shouted loud in some foreign tongue, but no mercy was shown them. We went ower them like a wave, and trampled them doon into the mud, for they were few, and there was no end to our numbers.

'I found myself among buildings, and one of them was on fire. I saw the flames spoutin' through the roof. I ran on, and then I was alone among the buildings. Someone ran across in front o' me. It was a woman. I caught her by the arm, and I took her chin and turned her face so as the light of the fire would strike it. Whom think you that it was, Maggie?'

His wife moistened her dry lips. 'It was I,' she said.

He looked at her in surprise. 'That's a good guess,' said he. 'Yes, it was just you. Not merely like you, you understand. It was you – you yourself. I saw the same soul in your frightened eyes. You looked white and bonny and wonderful in the firelight. I had just one thought in my head – to get you awa' with me; to keep you all to mysel' in my own home somewhere beyond the hills. You clawed at my face with your nails. I heaved you over my shoulder, and I tried to find a way oot of the light of the burning hoose and back into the darkness.

'Then came the thing that I mind best of all. You're ill, Maggie. Shall I stop? My God! you have the very look on your face that you had last night in my dream. You screamed. He came runnin' in the firelight. His head was bare; his hair was black and curled; he had a naked sword in his hand, short and broad, little more than a dagger. He stabbed at me, but he tripped and fell. I held you with one hand, and with the other –'

His wife had sprung to her feet with writhing features.

'Marcus!' she cried. 'My beautiful Marcus! Oh, you brute! you brute! you brute!' There was a clatter of teacups as she fell forward senseless upon the table.

They never talk about that strange isolated incident in their married life. For an instant the curtain of the past had swung aside, and some strange glimpse of a forgotten life had come to them. But it closed down, never to open again.

They live their narrow round – he in his shop, she in her household – and yet new and wider horizons have vaguely formed themselves around them since that summer evening by the crumbling Roman fort.

Part Four

A CLASSIC VICTORIAN
FAIRY TALE

THE GOLD OF FAIRNILEE
Andrew Lang

Chapter I:
THE OLD HOUSE

You may still see the old Scots house where Randal was born, so long ago. Nobody lives there now. Most of the roof has fallen in, there is no glass in the windows, and all the doors are open. They were open in the days of Randal's father – nearly five hundred years have passed since then – and everyone who came was welcome to his share of beef and broth and ale. But now the doors are not only open, they are quite gone, and there is nobody within to give you a welcome.

So there is nothing but emptiness in the old house where Randal lived with Jean, four hundred and sixty years or so before you were born. It is a high old house, and wide, with the broken slates still on the roof. At the corner there are little round towers, like pepperboxes, with sharp peaks. The stems of the ivy that covers the walls are as thick as trees.

There are many trees crowding all round, and there are hills round it too; and far below you hear the Tweed whispering all day. The house is called Fairnilee, which means 'the Fairies' Field'; for people believed in fairies, as you shall hear, when Randal was a boy, and even when my father was a boy.

Randal was all alone in the house when he was a little fellow – alone with his mother, and Nancy the old nurse, and Simon Grieve the butler, who wore a black velvet coat and a big silver chain. Then there were the maids, and the grooms, and the farm folk, who were all friends of Randal's. He was not lonely, and he did not feel unhappy, even before Jean came, as you shall be told. But the grown-up people were sad and silent at Fairnilee. Randal had no father; his mother, Lady Ker, was a widow. She was still quite young, and Randal thought her the most beautiful person in the world. Children think these things about their mothers, and Randal had seen no ladies but his mother only. She had brown hair and brown eyes and red lips, and a grave kind face, which looked serious under her great white widow's cap with the black hood over it. Randal never saw his mother cry; but when he was a very little child indeed, he had heard her crying in the night: this was after his father went away.

Chapter II:
HOW RANDAL'S FATHER CAME HOME

Randal remembered his father going to fight the English, and how he came back again. It was a windy August evening when he went away: the rain had fallen since morning. Randal had watched the white mists driven by the gale down through the black pine wood that covers the hill opposite Fairnilee. The mist looked like armies of ghosts, he thought, marching, marching through the pines, with their

white flags flying and streaming. Then the sun came out red at evening, and Randal's father rode away with all his men. He had a helmet on his head, and a great axe hanging from his neck by a chain, and a spear in his hand. He was riding his big horse, Sir Hugh, and he caught Randal up to the saddle and kissed him many times before he clattered out of the courtyard. All the tenants and men about the farm rode with him, all with spears and a flag embroidered with a crest in gold. His mother watched them from the tower till they were out of sight. And Randal saw them ride away, not on hard, smooth roads like ours, but along a green grassy track, the water splashing up to their stirrups where they crossed the marshes.

Then the sky turned as red as blood, in the sunset, and next it grew brown, like the rust on a sword; and the Tweed below, when they rode the ford, was all red and gold and brown.

Then time went on; that seemed a long time to Randal.

Only the women were left in the house, and Randal played with the shepherd's children. They sailed boats in the mill-pond, and they went down to the boat-pool and watched to see the big copper-coloured salmon splashing in the still water. One evening Randal looked up suddenly from his play. It was growing dark. He had been building a house with the round stones and wet sand by the river. He looked up, and there was his own father! He was riding all alone, and his horse, Sir Hugh, was very lean and lame, and scarred with the spurs. The spear in his father's hand was broken, and he had no sword; and he looked neither to right nor to left. His eyes were wide open, but he seemed to see nothing.

Randal cried out to him, 'Father! Father!' but he never glanced at Randal. He did not look as if he heard him; or knew he was there, and suddenly he seemed to go away, Randal did not know how or where.

Randal was frightened.

He ran into the house, and went to his mother.

'Oh, mother,' he said, 'I have seen father! He was riding all alone, and he would not look at me. Sir Hugh was lame!'

'Where has he gone?' said Lady Ker, in a strange voice.

'He went away out of sight,' said Randal. 'I could not see where he went.'

Then his mother told him it could not be, that his father would not have come back alone. He would not leave his men behind him in the war.

But Randal was so sure, that she did not scold him. She knew he believed what he said.

He saw that she was not happy.

All that night, which was the fourth of September, in the year 1513, the day of Flodden fight, Randal's mother did not go to bed. She kept moving about the house. Now she would look from the tower window up Tweed; and now she would go along the gallery and look down Tweed from the other tower.

She had lights burning in all the windows. All next day she was never still. She climbed, with two of her maids, to the top of the hill above Yair, on the other side of the river, and she watched the roads down Ettrick and Yarrow. Next night she slept little, and rose early. About noon, Randal saw three or four men riding wearily, with tired horses. They could scarcely cross the ford of Tweed, the horses were so tired. The men were Simon Grieve the butler, and some of the tenants. They looked very pale; some of them had their heads tied up, and there was blood on their faces. Lady Ker and Randal ran to meet them.

Simon Grieve lighted from his horse, and whispered to Randal's mother.

Randal did not hear what he said, but his mother cried, 'I knew it! I knew it!' and turned quite white.

'Where is he?' she said.

Simon pointed across the hill. 'They are bringing the corp,' he said. Randal knew 'the corp' meant the dead body.

He began to cry. 'Where is my father?' he said. 'Where is my father?'

His mother led him into the house. She gave him to the old nurse, who cried over him, and kissed him, and offered him cakes, and made him a whistle with a branch of plane tree. So in a short while Randal only felt puzzled. Then he forgot, and began to play. He was a very little boy.

Lady Ker shut herself up in her own room – her 'bower', the servants called it.

Soon Randal heard heavy steps on the stairs, and whispering. He wanted to run out, and his nurse caught hold of him, and would not have let him go, but he slipped out of her hand, and looked over the staircase.

They were bringing up the body of a man stretched on a shield.

It was Randal's father.

He had been slain at Flodden, fighting for the king. An

arrow had gone through his brain, and he had fallen beside James IV, with many another brave knight, all the best of Scotland, the Flowers of the Forest.

What was it Randal had seen, when he thought he met his father in the twilight, three days before?

He never knew. His mother said he must have dreamed it all.

The old nurse used to gossip about it to the maids. 'He's an unco' bairn, oor Randal; I wush he may na be fey.'

She meant that Randal was a strange child, and that strange things would happen to him.

Chapter III:
HOW JEAN WAS BROUGHT TO FAIRNILEE

The winter went by very sadly. At first the people about Fairnilee expected the English to cross the Border and march against them. They drove their cattle out on the wild hills, and into marshes where only they knew the firm paths, and raised walls of earth and stones – *barmkyns*, they called them – round the old house; and made many arrows to shoot out of the narrow windows at the English. Randal used to like to see the arrow-making beside the fire at night. He was not afraid; and said he would show the English what he could do with his little bow. But weeks went on and no enemy came. Spring drew near, the snow melted from the hills. One night Randal was awakened by a great noise of shouting; he looked out of the window, and saw bright torches moving about. He heard the cows 'routing', or bellowing, and the women screaming. He thought the English had come. So they had; not the English army, but some robbers from the other side of the Border. At that time the people on the south side of Scotland and the north side of England used to steal each other's cows time about. When a Scots squire, or 'laird', like Randal's father, had been robbed by the neighbouring English, he would wait his chance and drive away cattle from the English side. This time most of Randal's mother's herds were seized, by a sudden attack in the night, and were driven away through the forest to England. Two or three of Lady Ker's men were hurt by the English, but old Simon Grieve took a prisoner. He did this in a curious way. He shot an arrow after the robbers as they rode off, and the arrow pinned an Englishman's leg to the saddle, and even into his horse. The horse was hurt and frightened, and ran away right back to Fairnilee, where it was caught, with the rider and all, for of course he could not dismount.

They treated him kindly at Fairnilee, though they laughed at him a good deal. They found out from him where the English had come from. He did not mind telling them, for he was really a gypsy from Yetholm, where the gypsies live, and Scot or Southron was all one to him.

When old Simon Grieve knew who the people were that

had taken the cows, he was not long in calling the men together, and trying to get back what he had lost. Early one April morning, a grey morning, with snow in the air, he and his spearmen set out, riding down through the forest, and so into Liddesdale. When they came back again, there were great rejoicings at Fairnilee. They drove most of their own cows before them, and a great many other cows that they had not lost; cows of the English farmers. The byres and yards were soon full of cattle, lowing and roaring, very uneasy, and some of them with marks of the spears that had goaded them across many a ford, and up many a rocky pass in the hills.

Randal jumped downstairs to the great hall, where his mother sat. Simon Grieve was telling her all about it.

'Sae we drave oor ain kye hame, my lady,' he said, 'and aiblins some orra anes that was na oor ain. For-bye we raikit a' the plenishing oot o' the ha' o' Hardriding, and a bonny burden o' tapestries, and plaids, and gear we hae, to show for our ride.'*

Then he called to some of his men, who came into the hall, and cast down great piles of all sorts of spoil and booty, silver plate, and silken hangings, and a heap of rugs, and carpets, and plaids, such as Randal had never seen before, for the English were much richer than the Scots.

Randal threw himself on the pile of rugs and began to roll on it.

'Oh, mother,' he cried suddenly, jumping up and looking with wide-open eyes, 'there's something living in the heap! Perhaps it's a doggie, or a rabbit, or a kitten.'

Then Randal tugged at the cloths, and then they all heard a little shrill cry.

* 'We drove our own cattle home, and perhaps some others that were not ours. And we took all the goods out of the hall at Hardriding, and a pretty load of tapestries, and rugs, and other things we have to show for our ride.'

'Why, it's a bairn!' said Lady Ker, who had sat very grave all the time, pleased to have done the English some harm; for they had killed her husband, and were all her deadly foes. 'It's a bairn!' she cried, and pulled out of the great heap of cloaks and rugs a little beautiful child, in its white nightdress, with its yellow curls all tangled over its blue eyes.

Then Lady Ker and the old nurse could not make too much of the pretty English child that had come here in such a wonderful way.

How did it get mixed up with all the spoil? And how had it been carried so far on horseback without being hurt? Nobody ever knew. It came as if the fairies had sent it. English it was, but the best Scot could not hate such a pretty child. Old Nancy Dryden ran up to the old nursery with it, and laid it in a great wooden tub full of hot water, and was giving it warm milk to drink, and dandling it, almost before the men knew what had happened.

'Yon bairn will be a bonny mate for you, Maister Randal,' said old Simon Grieve. 'Deed, I dinna think her kin will come speering* after her at Fairnilee. The red cock's crawing ower Hardriding Ha' this day, and when the womenfolk come back frae the wood, they'll hae other things to do forbye looking for bairns.'

When Simon Grieve said that the red cock was crowing over his enemies' home, he meant that he had set it on fire after the people who lived in it had run away.

Lady Ker grew pale when she heard what he said. She hated the English, to be sure, but she was a woman with a kind heart. She thought of the dreadful danger that the little English girl had escaped, and she went upstairs and helped the nurse to make the child happy.

* Asking

Chapter IV:
RANDAL AND JEAN

The little girl soon made everyone at Fairnilee happy. She was far too young to remember her own home, and presently she was crawling up and down the long hall and making friends with Randal. They found out that her name was Jane Musgrave, though she could hardly say Musgrave; and they called her Jean, with their Scots tongues, or 'Jean o' the Kye', because she came when the cows were driven home again.

Soon the old nurse came to like her near as well as Randal, 'her ain bairn' (her own child), as she called him. In the summer days, Jean, as she grew older, would follow Randal about like a little doggie. They went fishing together, and Randal would pull the trout out of Caddon Burn, or the Burn of Peel; and Jeanie would be very proud of him, and very much alarmed at the big, wide jaws of the yellow trout. And Randal would plait helmets with green rushes for her and him, and make spears of bulrushes, and play at tilts and tournaments. There was peace in the country; or if there was war, it did not come near the quiet valley of the Tweed and the hills that lie round Fairnilee. In summer they were always on the hills and by the burnsides.

You cannot think, if you have not tried, what pleasant company a burn is. It comes out of the deep, black wells in the moss, far away on the tops of the hills, where the sheep feed, and the fox peers from his hole, and the ravens build in the crags. The burn flows down from the lonely places, cutting a way between steep, green banks, tumbling in white waterfalls over rocks, and lying in black, deep pools below the waterfalls. At every turn it does something new and plays a fresh game with its brown waters. The white pebbles in the water look like gold: often Randal would pick one out and think he had found a gold-mine, till he got it into the sunshine, and then it was only a white stone, what he called a 'chucky-stane'; but he kept hoping for better luck next time. In the height of summer, when the streams were very low, he and the shepherd's boys would build dams of stones and turf across a narrow part of the burn, while Jean sat and watched them on a little round knoll. Then, when plenty of water had collected in the pool, they would break the dam and let it all run downhill in a little flood; they called it a 'hurly gush'. And in winter they would slide on the black, smooth ice of the boat-pool, beneath the branches of the alders.

Or they would go out with Yarrow, the shepherd's dog, and follow the track of wild creatures in the snow. The rabbit makes marks like this ˙·˙, and the hare makes marks like this ˙:˙; but the fox's track is just as if you had pushed a piece of wood through the snow – a number of cuts in the surface, going straight along. When it was very cold, the grouse and blackcocks would come into the trees near the house, and Randal and Jean would put out porridge for them to eat. And the great white swans floated in from the frozen lochs on the hills, and gathered round open reaches and streams of the Tweed. It was pleasant to be a boy then in the North. And at Hallowe'en they would duck for apples in tubs of water, and burn nuts in the fire, and look for the shadow of the lady Randal was to marry, in the mirror; but he only saw Jean looking over his shoulder.

The days were very short in winter, so far North, and they would soon be driven into the house. Then they sat by the nursery fire; and those were almost the pleasantest hours, for the old nurse would tell them old Scots stories of elves and fairies, and sing them old songs. Jean would crawl close to Randal and hold his hand, for fear the Red Etin, or some other awful bogle, should get her; and in the dancing shadows of the firelight she would think she saw Whuppity Stoorie, the wicked old witch with the spinning-wheel; but it was really nothing but the shadow of the wheel that the old nurse drove with her foot – *birr, birr* – and that whirred and rattled as she span and told her tale. For people span their cloth at home then, instead of buying it from shops; and the old nurse was a great woman for spinning.

She was a great woman for stories, too, and believed in fairies, and 'bogles', as she called them. Had not her own cousin, Andrew Tamson, passed the Cauldshiels Loch one New Year morning? And had he not heard a dreadful roaring, as if all the cattle on Faldonside Hill were routing at once? And then did he not see a great black beast roll down the hillside, like a black ball, and run into the loch, which grew white with foam, and the waves leaped up the banks like a tide rising? What could that be except the kelpie that lives in Cauldshiels Loch, and is just a muckle big water bull? 'And what for should there no be water kye, if there's land kye?'

Randal and Jean thought it was very likely there were 'kye', or cattle, in the water. And some Highland people think so still, and believe they have seen the great kelpie come roaring out of the lake; or Shellycoat, whose skin is all crusted like a rock with shells, sitting beside the sea.

The old nurse had other tales, that nobody believes any longer, about Brownies. A Brownie was a very useful creature to have in a house. He was a kind of fairy-man, and he came out in the dark, when everybody had gone to bed, just as mice pop out at night. He never did anyone any harm, but he sat and warmed himself at the kitchen fire. If any work was unfinished he did it, and made everything tidy that was left out of order. It is a pity there are no such bogles now! If anybody offered the Brownie any payment, even if it was only a silver penny or a new coat, he would take offence and go away.

Other stories the old nurse had, about hidden treasures and buried gold. If you believed her, there was hardly an old stone on the hillside that didn't have gold under it. The very sheep that fed upon the Eildon Hills, which Randal knew well, had yellow teeth because there was so much gold under the grass. Randal had taken two scones, or rolls, in his pocket for dinner, and ridden over to the Eildon Hills. He had seen a rainbow touch one of them, and there he hoped he would find the treasure that always lies at the tail of the rainbow. But he got very soon tired of digging for it with his little dirk, or dagger. It blunted the dagger, and he found nothing. Perhaps he had not marked quite the right place, he thought. But he looked at the teeth of the sheep, and they were yellow; so he had no doubt that there was a gold-mine under the grass, if he could find it.

The old nurse knew that it was very difficult to dig up fairy gold. Generally something happened just when people heard their pickaxes clink on the iron pot that held the treasure. A dreadful storm of thunder and lightning would break out; or the burn would be flooded, and rush down all red and roaring, sweeping away the tools and drowning the digger; or a strange man, that nobody had ever seen before, would come up, waving his arms, and crying out that the Castle was on fire. Then the people would hurry up to the Castle, and find that it was not on fire at all. When they returned, all the earth would be just as it was before they began, and they would give up in despair. Nobody could ever see the man again that gave the alarm.

'Who could he be, nurse?' Randal asked.

'Just one of the good folk, I'm thinking; but it's no weel to be speaking o' *them*.'

Randal knew that the 'good folk' meant the fairies. The old nurse called them the good folk for fear of offending them. She would not speak much about them, except now and then, when the servants had been making merry.

'And is there any treasure hidden near Fairnilee, nursie?' asked little Jean.

'Treasure, my bonny doo! Mair than a' the men about the

toon could carry away frae morning till nicht. Do ye no ken the auld rhyme?

> *Atween the wet ground and the dry*
> *The gold of Fairnilee doth lie.*

'And there's the other auld rhyme:

> *Between the Camp o' Rink*
> *And Tweed-water clear,*
> *Lie nine kings' ransoms*
> *For nine hundred year!'*

Randal and Jean were very glad to hear so much gold was near them as would pay nine kings' ransoms. They took their small spades and dug little holes in the Camp of Rink, which is a great old circle of stonework, surrounded by a deep ditch, on the top of a hill above the house. But Jean was not a very good digger, and even Randal grew tired. They thought they would wait till they grew bigger, and *then* find the gold.

Chapter V:
THE GOOD FOLK

'Everybody knows there's fairies,' said the old nurse one night when she was bolder than usual. What she said we will put in English, not Scots as she spoke it. 'But they do not like to be called fairies. So the old rhyme runs:

> *If ye call me imp or elf,*
> *I warn you look well to yourself;*
> *If ye call me fairy,*
> *Ye'll find me quite contrary;*
> *If good neighbour you call me,*

Then good neighbour I will be;
But if you call me kindly sprite,
I'll be your friend both day and night.

'So you must always call them "good neighbours" or "good folk", when you speak of them.'

'Did *you* ever see a fairy, nurse?' asked Randal.

'Not myself, but my mother knew a woman – they called her Tibby Dickson, and her husband was a shepherd, and she had a bairn, as bonny a bairn as ever you saw. And one day she went to the well to draw water, and as she was coming back she heard a loud scream in her house. Then her heart leaped, and fast she ran and flew to the cradle; and there she saw an awful sight – not her own bairn, but a withered imp, with hands like a mole's, and a face like a frog's, and a mouth from ear to ear, and two great staring eyes.'

'What was it?' asked Jeanie, in a trembling voice.

'A fairy's bairn that had not thriven,' said nurse; 'and when their bairns do not thrive, they just steal honest folk's children and carry them away to their own country.'

'And where's that?' asked Randal.

'It's under the ground,' said nurse, 'and there they have gold and silver and diamonds; and there's the Queen of them all, that's as beautiful as the day. She has yellow hair down to her feet, and she has blue eyes, like the sky on a fine day, and her voice like all the mavises singing in the spring. And she is aye dressed in green, and all her court in green; and she rides a white horse with golden bells on the bridle.'

'I would like to go there and see her,' said Randal.

'Oh, never say that, my bairn; you never know who may hear you! And if you go there, how will you come back again? And what will your mother do, and Jean here, and me that's carried you many a time in weary arms when you were a babe?'

'Can't people come back again?' asked Randal.

'Some say "Yes", and some say "No". There was Tam Hislop, that vanished away the day before all the lads and your own father went forth to that weary war at Flodden, and the English, for once, by guile, won the day. Well, Tam Hislop, when the news came that all must arm and mount and ride, he could nowhere be found. It was as if the wind had carried him away. High and low they sought him, but there was his clothes and his armour, and his sword and his spear, but no Tam Hislop. Well, no man heard more of him for seven whole years, not till last year, and then he came back: sore tired he looked, ay, and older than when he was lost. And I met him by the well, and I was frightened; and, "Tam," I said, "where have ye been this weary time?" "I have been with them that I will not speak the name of," says he. "Ye mean the good folk," said I. "Ye have said it," says he. Then I went up to the house, with my heart in my mouth, and I met Simon Grieve. "Simon," I says, "here's Tam Hislop come home from the good folk." "I'll soon send him back to them," says he. And he takes a great stick and lays it about Tam's shoulders, calling him coward loon, that ran away from the fighting. And since then Tam has never been seen about the place. But the Laird's man, of Gala, knows them that say Tam was in Perth the last seven years, and not in Fairyland at all. But it was Fairyland he told me, and he would not lie to his own mother's half-brother's cousin.'

Randal did not care much for the story of Tam Hislop. A fellow who would let old Simon Grieve beat him could not be worthy of the Fairy Queen.

Randal was about thirteen now, a tall boy, with dark eyes, black hair, a brown face with the red on his cheeks. He had grown up in a country where everything was magical and haunted; where fairy knights rode on the leas after dark, and challenged men to battle. Every castle had its tale of Redcap, the sly spirit, or of the woman of the hairy hand.

Every old mound was thought to cover hidden gold. And all
was so lonely; the green hills rolling between river and river,
with no men on them, nothing but sheep, and grouse, and
plover. No wonder that Randal lived in a kind of dream. He
would lie and watch the long grass till it looked like a
forest, and he thought he could see elves dancing between
the green grass stems, that were like fairy trees. He kept
wishing that he, too, might meet the Fairy Queen, and be
taken into that other world where everything was beautiful.

Chapter VI:
THE WISHING WELL

'Jean,' said Randal one midsummer day, 'I am going to the
Wishing Well.'

'Oh, Randal,' said Jean, 'it is so far away!'

'I can walk it,' said Randal, 'and you must come, too; I
want you to come, Jeanie. It's not so very far.'

'But mother says it is wrong to go to Wishing Wells,' Jean
answered.

'Why is it wrong?' said Randal, switching at the tall
foxgloves with a stick.

'Oh, she says it is a wicked thing, and forbidden by the
Church. People who go to wish there, sacrifice to the spirits
of the well; and Father Francis told her that it was very
wrong.'

'Father Francis is a shaveling,' said Randal. 'I heard
Simon Grieve say so.'

'What's a shaveling, Randal?'

'I don't know: a man that does not fight, I think. I don't
care what a shaveling says: so I mean just to go and wish,
and I won't sacrifice anything. There can't be any harm in
that!'

'But, oh, Randal, you've got your green doublet on!'

'Well! Why not?'

'Do you not know it angers the fair – I mean the good folk – that anyone should wear green on the hill but themselves?'

'I cannot help it,' said Randal. 'If I go in and change my doublet, they will ask what I do that for. I'll chance it, green or grey, and wish my wish for all that.'

'And what are you going to wish?'

'I'm going to wish to meet the Fairy Queen! Just think how beautiful she must be, dressed all in green, with gold bells on her bridle, and riding a white horse shod with gold! I think I see her galloping through the woods and out across the hill, over the heather.'

'But you will go away with her, and never see me any more,' said Jean.

'No, I won't; or if I do, I'll come back, with such a horse, and a sword with a gold handle. I'm going to the Wishing Well. Come on!'

Jean did not like to say 'No', so off they went.

Randal and Jean started without taking anything with them to eat. They were afraid to go back to the house for food. Randal said they would be sure to find something somewhere. The Wishing Well was on the top of a hill between Yarrow and Tweed. So they took off their shoes, and waded the Tweed at the shallowest part, and then they walked up the green grassy bank on the other side, till they came to the Burn of Peel. Here they passed the old square tower of Peel, and the shepherd dogs came out and barked at them. Randal threw a stone at them, and they ran away with their tails between their legs.

'Don't you think we had better go into Peel, and get some bannocks to eat on the way, Randal?' said Jean.

But Randal said he was not hungry; and, besides, the people at Peel would tell the Fairnilee people where they had gone.

'We'll *wish* for things to eat when we get to the Wishing Well,' said Randal. 'All sorts of good things – cold venison pasty, and everything you like.'

So they began climbing the hill, and they followed the Peel Burn. It ran in and out, winding this way and that, and when they did get to the top of the hill, Jean was very tired and very hungry. And she was very disappointed. For she expected to see some wonderful new country at her feet, and there was only a low strip of sunburnt grass and heather, and then another hill-top! So Jean sat down, and the hot sun blazed on her, and the flies buzzed about her and tormented her.

'Come on, Jean,' said Randal; 'it must be over the next hill!'

So poor Jean got up and followed him, but he walked far too fast for her. When she reached the crest of the next hill, she found a great cairn, or pile of grey stones; and beneath her lay, far, far below, a deep valley covered with woods, and a stream running through it that she had never seen before.

That stream was the Yarrow.

Randal was nowhere in sight, and she did not know where to look for the Wishing Well. If she had walked straight forward through the trees she would have come to it; but she was so tired, and so hungry, and so hot, that she sat down at the foot of the cairn and cried as if her heart would break.

Then she fell asleep.

When Jean woke, it was as dark as it ever is on a midsummer night in Scotland.

It was a soft, cloudy night; not a clear night with a silver sky.

Jeanie heard a loud roaring close to her, and the red light of a great fire was in her sleepy eyes.

In the firelight she saw strange black beasts, with horns,

167

plunging and leaping and bellowing, and dark figures rushing about the flames. It was the beasts that made the roaring. They were bounding about close to the fire, and sometimes in it, and were all mixed in the smoke.

Jeanie was dreadfully frightened, too frightened to scream.

Presently she heard the voices of men shouting on the hill below her. The shouts and the barking of dogs came nearer and nearer.

Then a dog ran up to her, and licked her face, and jumped about her.

It was her own sheep-dog, Yarrow.

He ran back to the men who were following him, and came again with one of them.

It was old Simon Grieve, very tired, and so much out of breath that he could scarcely speak.

Jean was very glad to see him, and not frightened any longer.

'Oh, Jeanie, my doo,' said Simon, 'where hae ye been? A muckle gliff ye hae gien us, and a weary spiel up the weary braes.'

Jean told him all about it: how she had come with Randal to see the Wishing Well, and how she had lost him, and fallen asleep.

'And sic a nicht for you bairns to wander on the hill,' said Simon. 'It's the nicht o' St John, when the guid folk hae power. And there's a' the lads burning the Bel fires, and driving the nowt (cattle) through them: nae less will serve them. Sic a nicht!'

This was the cause of the fire Jean saw, and of the noise of the cattle. On Midsummer Night the country people used to light these fires, and drive the cattle through them. It was an old, old custom come down from heathen times.

Now the other men from Fairnilee had gathered round Jean. Lady Ker had sent them out to look for Randal and her on the hills. They had heard from the good wife at Peel that the children had gone up the burn, and Yarrow had tracked them till Jean was found.

Chapter VII:
WHERE IS RANDAL?

Jean was found, but where was Randal? She told the men who had come out to look for her, that Randal had gone on to look for the Wishing Well. So they rolled her up in a big shepherd's plaid, and two of them carried Jean home in the plaid, while all the rest, with lighted torches in their hands, went to look for Randal through the wood.

Jean was so tired that she fell asleep again in her plaid before they reached Fairnilee. She was wakened by the men shouting as they drew near the house, to show that they were coming home. Lady Ker was waiting at the gate, and the old nurse ran down the grassy path to meet them.

'Where's my bairn?' she cried as soon as she was within call.

The men said, 'Here's Mistress Jean, and Randal will be here soon; they have gone to look for him.'

'Where are they looking?' cried nurse.

'Just about the Wishing Well.'

The nurse gave a scream, and hobbled back to Lady Ker.

'Ma bairn's tint (lost)!' she cried. 'Ma bairn's tint! They'll find him never. The good folk have stolen him away from that weary Wishing Well!'

'Hush, nurse,' said Lady Ker, 'do not frighten Jean.'

She spoke to the men, who had no doubt that Randal would soon be found and brought home.

So Jean was put to bed, where she forgot all her troubles; and Lady Ker waited, waited, all night, till the grey light began to come in, about two in the morning.

Lady Ker kept very still and quiet, telling her beads, and praying. But the old nurse would never be still, but was always wandering out, down to the river's edge, listening for the shouts of the shepherds coming home. Then she would come back again, and moan and wring her hands, crying for her 'bairn'.

About six o'clock, when it was broad daylight and all the birds were singing, the men returned from the hill.

But Randal did not come with them.

Then the old nurse set up a great cry, as the country people do over the bed of someone who has just died.

Lady Ker sent her away, and called Simon Grieve to her own room.

'You have not found the boy yet?' she said, very stately and pale. 'He must have wandered over into Yarrow; perhaps he has gone as far as Newark, and passed the night at the castle, or with the shepherd at Foulshiels.'

'No, my Lady,' said Simon Grieve, 'some o' the men went over to Newark, and some to Foulshiels, and other some down to Sir John Murray's at Philiphaugh; but there's never a word o' Randal in a' the countryside.'

'Did you find no trace of him?' said Lady Ker, sitting down suddenly in the great armchair.

'We went first through the wood, my Lady, by the path to the Wishing Well. And he had been there, for the whip he carried in his hand was lying on the grass. And we found *this*.'

He put his hand in his pouch, and brought out a little silver crucifix, that Randal used always to wear round his neck on a chain.

'This was lying on the grass beside the Wishing Well, my Lady –'

Then he stopped, for Lady Ker had swooned away. She was worn out with watching and with anxiety about Randal.

Simon went and called the maids, and they brought water and wine, and soon Lady Ker came back to herself, with the little silver crucifix in her hand.

The old nurse was crying, and making a great noise.

'The good folk have taken ma bairn,' she said, 'this nicht o' a' the nichts in the year, when the fairy folk – preserve us frae them! – have power. But they could nae take the blessed rood o' grace; it was beyond their strength. If gypsies, or robber folk frae the Debatable Land, had carried away the bairn, they would hae taken him, cross and a'. But the guid folk have gotten him, and Randal Ker will never, never mair come hame to bonny Fairnilee.'

What the old nurse said was what everybody thought. Even Simon Grieve shook his head, and did not like it.

But Lady Ker did not give up hope. She sent horsemen through all the countryside: up Tweed to the Crook, and to Talla; up Yarrow, past Catslack Tower, and on to the Loch of Saint Mary; up Ettrick to Thirlestane and Buccleuch, and over to Gala, and to Branxholme in Teviotdale; and even to Hermitage Castle, far away by Liddel water.

They rode far and rode fast, and at every cottage and every tower they asked, 'Has anyone seen a boy in green?' But nobody had seen Randal through all the countryside.

Only a shepherd lad, on Foulshiels Hill, had heard bells ringing in the night, and a sound of laughter go past him, like a breeze of wind over the heather.

Days went by, and all the country was out to look for Randal. Down in Yetholm they sought him, among the gypsies; and across the Eden in merry Carlisle; and through the Land Debatable, where the robber Armstrongs and Grahames lived; and far down Tweed, past Melrose, and up Jed water, far into the Cheviot Hills.

But there never came any word of Randal. He had vanished as if the earth had opened and swallowed him. Father Francis came from Melrose Abbey, and prayed with Lady Ker, and gave her all the comfort he could. He shook his head when he heard of the Wishing Well, but he said that no spirit of earth or air could have power for ever over a Christian soul. But, even when he spoke, he remembered that, once in seven years, the fairy folk have to pay a dreadful tax, one of themselves, to the King of a terrible country of Darkness; and what if they had stolen Randal, to pay the tax with him!

This was what troubled good Father Francis, though, like a wise man, he said nothing about it, and even put the thought away out of his own mind.

But you may be sure that the old nurse had thought of this tax on the fairies too, and that *she* did not hold her peace about it, but spoke to everyone that would listen to her, and would have spoken to the mistress if she had been allowed. But when she tried to begin, Lady Ker told her that she had put her own trust in Heaven, and in the Saints. And she gave the nurse such a look when she said that, 'if ever Jean hears of this, I will send you away from Fairnilee, out of the country,' that the old woman was afraid, and was quiet.

As for poor Jean, she was perhaps the most unhappy of them all. She thought to herself, if she had refused to go with Randal to the Wishing Well, and had run in and told Lady Ker, then Randal would never have gone to find the Wishing Well.

And she put herself in great danger, as she fancied, to find him. She wandered alone on the hills, seeking all the places that were believed to be haunted by fairies. At every Fairy Knowe, as the country people called the little round green knolls in the midst of the heather, Jean would stoop her ear to the ground, trying to hear the voices of the fairies within. For it was believed that you might hear the sound of their speech, and the trampling of their horses, and the shouts of the fairy children. But no sound came, except the song of the burn flowing by, and the hum of gnats in the air, and the *gock, gock,* the cry of the grouse, when you frighten them in the heather.

Then Jeanie would try another way of meeting the fairies, and finding Randal. She would walk nine times round a Fairy Knowe, beginning from the left side, because then it was fancied that the hillside would open, like a door, and show a path into Fairyland. But the hillside never opened, and she never saw a single fairy; not even old Whuppity Stoorie sitting with her spinning-wheel in a green glen, spinning grass into gold, and singing her fairy song:

> '*I once was young and fair,*
> *My eyes were bright and blue,*
> *As if the sun shone through,*
> *And golden was my hair.*
>
> *Down to my feet it rolled*
> *Ruddy and ripe like corn,*
> *Upon an autumn morn,*
> *In heavy waves of gold.*
>
> *Now am I grey and old,*
> *And so I sit and spin,*

With trembling hand and thin,
This metal bright and cold.

I would give all the gain,
These heaps of wealth untold
Of hard and glittering gold,
Could I be young again!'

Chapter VIII:
THE ILL YEARS

So autumn came, and all the hillsides were golden with the heather; and the red coral berries of the rowan trees hung from the boughs, and were wet with the spray of the waterfalls in the burns. And days grew shorter, and winter came with snow, but Randal never came back to Fairnilee. Season after season passed, and year after year. Lady Ker's hair grew white like snow, and her face thin and pale – for she fasted often, as was the rule of her Church; all this was before the Reformation. And she slept little, praying half the night for Randal's sake. And she went on pilgrimages to many shrines of the Saints: to St Boswells and St Rules, hard by the great Cathedral of St Andrews on the sea. Nay, she went across the Border as far as the Abbey of St Albans, and even to St Thomas's shrine of Canterbury, taking Jean with her. Many a weary mile they rode over hill and dale, and many an adventure they had, and ran many dangers from robbers, and soldiers disbanded from the wars.

But at last they had to come back to Fairnilee; and a sad place it was, and silent without the sound of Randal's voice in the hall, and the noise of his hunting-horn in the woods. None of the people wore mourning for him, though they mourned in their hearts. For to put on black would look as if they had given up all hope. Perhaps most of them thought they would never see him again, but Jeanie was not one who despaired.

The years that had turned Lady Ker's hair white, had made Jean a tall, slim lass – 'very bonny', everyone said; and the country people called her the Flower of Tweed. The Yarrow folk had their Flower of Yarrow, and why not the folk of Tweedside? It was now six years since Randal had been lost, and Jeanie was grown a young woman, about seventeen years old. She had always kept a hope that if Randal was with the Fairy Queen he would return perhaps in the seventh year. People said in the countryside that many a man and woman had escaped out of Fairyland after seven years' imprisonment there.

Now the sixth year since Randal's disappearance began very badly, and got worse as it went on. Just when spring should have been beginning, in the end of February, there came the most dreadful snowstorm. It blew and snowed, and blew again, and the snow was as fine as the dust on a road in summer. The strongest shepherds could not hold their own against the tempest, and were 'smoored' (or smothered) in the waste. The flocks moved down from the hillsides, down and down, till all the sheep on a farm would be gathered together in a crowd, under the shelter of a wood in some deep dip of the hills. The storm seemed as if it would never cease; for thirteen days the snow drifted and the wind blew. There was nothing for the sheep to eat, and if there had been hay enough, it would have been impossible to carry it to them. The poor beasts bit at the wool on each other's backs, and so many of them died that the shepherds built walls with the dead bodies to keep the wind and snow away from those that were left alive.

There could be little work done on the farm that spring; and summer came in so cold and wet that the corn could not ripen, but was levelled to the ground. Then autumn was rainy, and the green sheaves lay out in the fields, and sprouted and rotted; so that little corn was reaped, and little flour could be made that year. Then in winter, and as spring came on, the people began to starve. They had no grain, and there were no potatoes in those days, and no rice; nor could corn be brought in from foreign countries. So men and women and children might be seen in the fields, with white pinched faces, gathering nettles to make soup, and digging for roots that were often little better than poison. They ground the bark of the fir trees, and mixed it with the little flour they could get; and they ate such beasts as never are eaten except in time of famine.

It is said that one very poor woman and her daughter always looked healthy and plump in these dreadful times, till people began to suspect them of being witches. And they were taken, and charged before the Sheriff with living by witchcraft, and very likely they would have been burned. So they confessed that they had fed ever since the famine began – on snails! But there were not snails enough for all the countryside; even if people had cared to eat them. So many men and women died, and more were very weak and ill.

Lady Ker spent all her money in buying food for her people. Jean and she lived on as little as they could, and were as careful as they could be. They sold all the beautiful silver plate, except the cup that Randal's father used to drink out of long ago. But almost everything else was sold to buy corn.

So the weary year went on, and Midsummer Night came round – the seventh since the night when Randal was lost.

Then Jean did what she had always meant to do. In the afternoon she slipped out of the house of Fairnilee, taking a little bread in a basket, and saying that she would go to see the farmer's wife at Peel, which was on the other side of Tweed. But her mind was to go to the Wishing Well. There she would wish for Randal back again, to help his mother in the evil times. And if she, too, passed away as he had passed out of sight and hearing, then at least she might meet him in that land where he had been carried. How strange it seemed to Jean to be doing everything over again that she had done seven years before! Then she had been a little girl, and it had been hard work for her to climb up the side of the Peel Burn. Now she walked lightly and quickly, for she was tall and well-grown. Soon she reached the crest of the first hill, and remembered how she had sat down there and cried, when she was a child, and how the flies had tormented her. They were buzzing and teasing still; for good times or bad make no difference to them, as long as the sun shines. Then she reached the cairn at the top of the next hill, and far below her lay the forest, and deep within it ran the Yarrow, glittering like silver.

Jean paused a few moments, and then struck into a green path which led through the wood. The path wound beneath dark pines; their top-most branches were red in the evening light, but the shade was black beneath them. Soon the path reached a little grassy glade, and there among cold, wet grasses was the Wishing Well. It was almost hidden by the grass, and looked very black, and cool, and deep. A tiny trickle of water flowed out of it and flowed down to join the Yarrow. The trees about it had scraps of rags and other things pinned to them, offerings made by the country people to the spirit of the well.

Chapter IX:
THE WHITE ROSES

Jeanie sat down beside the well. She wished her three wishes: to see Randal, to win him back from Fairyland, and to help the people in the famine. Then she knelt on the grass, and looked down into the well-water. At first she saw nothing but the smooth black water, with little waves trembling in it. Then the water began to grow bright within, as if the sun was shining far, far below. Then it grew as clear as crystal, and she saw through it, like a glass, into a new country – a beautiful country with a wide green plain, and in the midst of the plain a great castle, with golden flags floating from the tops of all the towers. Then she heard a curious whispering noise that thrilled and murmured, as if the music of all the trees that the wind blows through the world were in her ears, as if the noise of all the waves of every sea, and the rustling of heather-bells on every hill, and the singing of all birds were sounding, low and sweet, far, far away. Then she saw a great company of knights and ladies, dressed in green, ride up to the castle; and one knight rode apart from the rest, on a milk-white steed. They all went into the castle gates; but this knight rode slowly and sadly behind the others, with his head bowed on his breast.

Then the musical sounds were still, and the castle and the plain seemed to waver in the water. Next they quite vanished, and the well grew dim, and then grew dark and black and smooth as it had been before. Still she looked, and the little well bubbled up with sparkling foam, and so became still again, like a mirror, till Jeanie could see her own face in it, and beside her face came the reflection of another face, a young man's, dark, and sad, and beautiful. The lips smiled at her, and then Jeanie knew it was Randal. She thought he must be looking over her shoulder, and she leaped up with a cry, and glanced round.

But she was all alone, and the wood about her was empty and silent. The light had gone out of the sky, which was pale like silver, and overhead she saw the evening star.

Then Jeanie thought all was over. She had seen Randal as if it had been in a glass, and she hardly knew him: he was so much older, and his face was so sad. She sighed, and turned to go away over the hills, back to Fairnilee.

But her feet did not seem to carry her the way she wanted to go. It seemed as if something within her were moving her in a kind of dream. She felt herself going on through the forest, she did not know where. Deeper into the wood she went, and now it grew so dark that she saw scarcely anything; only she felt the fragrance of brier-roses, and it seemed to her that she was guided towards these roses. Then she knew there was a hand in her hand, though she saw nobody, and the hand seemed to lead her on. And she came to an open place in the forest, and there the silver light fell clear from the sky, and she saw a great shadowy rose tree, covered with white wild roses.

The hand was still in her hand, and Jeanie began to wish for nothing so much in the world as to gather some of these roses. She put out her hand and she plucked one, and there before her stood a strange creature – a dwarf, dressed in yellow and red, with a very angry face.

'Who are you,' he cried, 'that pluck my roses without my will?'

'And who are *you*?' said Jeanie, trembling, 'and what right have you on the hills of this world?'

Then she made the holy sign of the cross, and the face of the elf grew black, and the light went out of the sky.

She only saw the faint glimmer of the white flowers, and a kind of shadow standing where the dwarf stood.

'I bid you tell me,' said Jeanie, 'whether you are a Christian man, or a spirit that dreads the holy sign,' and she crossed him again.

Now all grew dark as the darkest winter's night. The air was warm and deadly still, and heavy with the scent of the fairy flowers.

In the blackness and the silence, Jeanie made the sacred sign for the third time. Then a clear fresh wind blew on her face, and the forest boughs were shaken, and the silver light grew and gained on the darkness, and she began to see a shape standing where the dwarf had stood. It was far taller than the dwarf, and the light grew and grew, and a star looked down out of the night, and Jean saw Randal standing by her. And she kissed him, and he kissed her, and he put

179

his hand in hers, and they went out of the wood together. They came to the crest of the hill and the cairn. Far below them they saw the Tweed shining through an opening among the trees, and the lights in the farm of Peel, and they heard the night-birds crying, and the bells of the sheep ringing musically as they wandered through the fragrant heather on the hills.

Chapter X:
OUT OF FAIRYLAND

You may fancy, if you can, what joy there was in Fairnilee when Randal came home. They quite forgot the hunger and the hard times, and the old nurse laughed and cried over her bairn that had grown into a tall, strong young man. And to Lady Ker it was all one as if her husband had come again, as he was when first she knew him long ago; for Randal had his face, and his eyes, and the very sound of his voice. They could hardly believe he was not a spirit, and they clasped his hands, and hung on his neck, and could not keep their eyes off him. This was the end of all their sorrow, and it was as if Randal had come back from the dead; so that no people in the world were ever so happy as they were next day, when the sun shone down on the Tweed and the green trees that rustle in the wind round Fairnilee. But in the evening, when the old nurse was out of the way, Randal sat between his mother and Jean, and they each held his hands, as if they could not let him go, for fear he should vanish away from them again. And they would turn round anxiously if anything stirred, for fear it should be the two white deer that sometimes were said to come for people escaped from Fairyland, and then these people must rise and follow them, and never return any more. But the white deer never came for Randal.

So he told them all his adventures, and all that had happened to him since that Midsummer Night, seven long years ago.

It had been with him as it was with Jean. He had gone to the Wishing Well, and wished to see the Fairy Queen and Fairyland. And he had seen the beautiful castle in the well, and a beautiful woman's face had floated up to meet his on the water. Then he had gathered the white roses, and then he heard a great sound of horses' feet, and of bells jingling, and a lady rode up, the very lady he had seen in the well. She had a white horse, and she was dressed in green, and she beckoned to Randal to mount on her horse, with her before him on the pillion. And the bells on the bridle rang, and the horse flew faster than the wind.

So they rode and rode through the summer night, and they came to a desert place, and living lands were left far behind. Then the Fairy Queen showed him three paths, one steep and narrow, and beset with briers and thorns: that was the road to goodness and happiness, but it was little trodden or marked with the feet of people that had come and gone.

And there was a wide smooth road that went through fields of lilies, and that was the path of easy living and pleasure.

The third path wound about the wild hillside, through ferns and heather, and that was the way to Elfland, and that way they rode. And still they rode through a country of dark night, and they crossed great black rivers, and they saw neither sun nor moon, but they heard the roaring of the sea. From that country they came into the light, and into the beautiful garden that lies round the castle of the Fairy Queen. There they lived in a noble company of gallant knights and fair ladies. All seemed very mirthful, and they rode, and hunted, and danced; and it was never dark night, nor broad daylight, but like early summer dawn before the sun has risen.

There Randal said that he had quite forgotten his mother and Jean, and the world where he was born, and Fairnilee.

But one day he happened to see a beautiful golden bottle of a strange shape, all set with diamonds, and he opened it. There was in it a sweet-smelling water, as clear as crystal, and he poured it into his hand, and passed his hand over his eyes. Now this water had the power to destroy the 'glamour' in Fairyland, and make people see it as it really was. And when Randal touched his eyes with it, lo, everything was changed in a moment. He saw that nothing was what it had seemed. The gold vanished from the embroidered curtains, the light grew dim and wretched like a misty winter day. The Fairy Queen, that had seemed so happy and beautiful in her bright dress, was a weary, pale woman in black, with a melancholy face and melancholy eyes. She looked as if she had been there for thousands of years, always longing for the sunlight and the earth, and the wind and rain. There were sleepy poppies twisted in her hair, instead of a golden crown. And the knights and ladies were changed. They looked but half alive; and some, in place of their bright green robes, were dressed in rusty mail, pierced with spears and stained with blood. And some were in burial robes of white, and some in dresses torn or dripping with water, or marked with the burning of fire. All were dressed strangely in some ancient fashion; their weapons were old-fashioned, too, unlike any that Randal had ever seen on earth. And their banquets were not of dainty meats, but of cold, tasteless flesh, and of beans, and pulse, and such things as the old heathens, before the coming of the Gospel, used to offer to the dead. It was dreadful to see them at such feasts, and dancing, and riding, and pretending to be merry with hollow faces and unhappy eyes.

And Randal wearied of Fairyland, which now that he saw it clearly looked like a great unending stretch of sand and barren grassy country, beside a grey sea where there was no tide. All the woods were of black cypress trees and poplar, and a wind from the sea drove a sea-mist through them, white and cold, and it blew through the open courts of the fairy castle.

So Randal longed more and more for the old earth he had left, and the changes of summer and autumn, and the streams of Tweed, and the hills, and his friends. Then the voice of Jeanie had come down to him, sounding from far away. And he was sent up by the Fairy Queen in a fairy form, as a hideous dwarf, to frighten her away from the white roses in the enchanted forest.

But her goodness and her courage had saved him, for he was a christened knight, and not a man of the fairy world. And he had taken his own form again beneath her hand, when she signed him with the Cross, and here he was, safe and happy, at home at Fairnilee.

Chapter XI:
THE FAIRY BOTTLE

We soon grow used to the greatest changes, and almost forget the things that we were accustomed to before. In a day or two, Randal had nearly forgotten what a dull life he had lived in Fairyland, after he had touched his eyes with the strange water in the fairy bottle. He remembered the long, grey sands, and the cold mist, and the white faces of the strange people, and the gloomy queen, no more than you remember the dream you dreamed a week ago. But he did notice that Fairnilee was not the happy place it had been before he went away. Here, too, the faces were pinched and white, and the people looked hungry. And he missed many things that he remembered: the silver cups, and plates, and tankards. And the dinners were not like they had been, but only a little thin soup, and some oatmeal cakes, and trout taken from the Tweed. The beef and ale of old times were not to be found, even in the houses of the richer people.

Very soon Randal heard all about the famine; you may be sure the old nurse was ready to tell him all the saddest stories.

> *Full many a place in evil case*
> *Where joy was wont afore, oh!*
> *Wi' Humes that dwell in Leader braes,*
> *And Scotts that dwell in Yarrow!*

And the old woman would croon her old prophecies, and tell them how Thomas the Rymer, that lived in Ercildoune, had foretold all this. And she would wish they could find these hidden treasures that the rhymes were full of, and that maybe were lying – who knew? – quite near them on their own lands.

'Where is the gold of Fairnilee?' she would cry; and, 'Oh,

Randal! can you no dig for it, and find it, and buy corn out of England for the poor folk that are dying at your doors?

> *Atween the wet ground and the dry*
> *The gold of Fairnilee doth lie!*

'There it is, with the sun never glinting on it; there it may bide, till the Judgment Day, and no man the better for it.

> *Between the Camp o' Rink*
> *And Tweed-water clear,*
> *Lie nine kings' ransoms*
> *For nine hundred year!'*

'I doubt it's fairy gold, nurse,' said Randal. It would all turn black when it saw the sun. It would just be like this bottle, the only thing I brought with me out of Fairyland.'

Then Randal put his hand in his velvet pouch, and brought out a curious small bottle. It was made of something that none of them had ever seen before. It was black, and you could see the light through it, and there were green and yellow spots and streaks on it. In bottles like this, the old Romans once kept their tears for their dead friends.

'That ugly bottle looked like gold and diamonds when I found it in Fairyland,' said Randal, 'and the water in it smelled as sweet as roses. But when I touched my eyes with it, a drop that ran into my mouth was as salt as the sea, and immediately everything changed: the gold bottle became this glass thing, and the fairies became like folk dead, and the sky grew grey, and all turned waste and ugly. That's the way with fairy gold, nurse; and even if you found it, it would all be dry leaves and black bits of coal before the sun set.'

'Maybe so, and maybe no,' said the old nurse. 'The gold o' Fairnilee may no be fairy gold, but just wealth o' this world that folk buried here lang syne. But noo, Randal, ma bairn, I maun gang out and see ma sister's son's dochter, that's lying sair sick o' the kin-cough (whooping cough) at Rink, and take her some of the medicine that I gae you and Jean when you were bairns.'

So the old nurse went out, and Randal and Jean began to be sorry for the child she was going to visit. For they remembered the taste of the medicine that the old nurse made by boiling the bark of elder-tree branches; and I remember it too, for it was the very nastiest thing that ever was tasted, and did nobody any good after all.

Then Randal and Jean walked out, strolling along without much noticing where they went, and talking about the pleasant days when they were children.

Chapter XII:
AT THE CATRAIL

They had climbed up the slope of a hill, and they came to a broad old ditch, beneath the shade of a wood of pine trees. Below them was a wide marsh, all yellow with marsh flowers, and above them was a steep slope made of stones. Now the dry ditch, where they sat down on the grass, looking towards the Tweed, with their backs to the hill, was called the Catrail. It ran all through that country, and must have been made by men very long ago. Nobody knows who made it, nor why. They did not know in Randal's time, and they do not know now. They do not even know what the name Catrail means, but that is what it has always been called. The steep slope of stone above them was named the Camp of Rink; it is a round place, like a ring, and no doubt it was built by the old Britons, when they fought against the Romans, many hundreds of years ago. The stones of which it is built are so large that we cannot tell how men moved them. But it is a very pleasant, happy place on a warm summer day, like the day when Randal and Jean sat there, with the daisies at their feet, and the wild doves cooing above their heads, and the rabbits running in and out among the ferns.

Jean and Randal talked about this and that, chiefly of how some money could be got to buy corn and cattle for the people. Randal was in favour of crossing the Border at night, and driving away cattle from the English side, according to the usual custom.

'Every day I expect to see a pair of spurs in a dish for all our dinner,' said Randal.

That was the sign the lady of the house in the forest used to give her men, when all the beef was done, and more had to be got by fighting.

But Jeanie would not hear of Randal taking spear and jack, and putting himself in danger by fighting the English. They were her own people after all, though she could not remember them and the days before she was carried out of England by Simon Grieve.

'Then,' said Randal, 'am I to go back to Fairyland, and fetch more gold like this ugly thing?' and he felt in his pocket for the fairy bottle.

But it was not in his pocket.

'What have I done with my fairy treasure?' cried Randal, jumping up. Then he stood still quite suddenly, as if he saw something strange. He touched Jean on the shoulder, making a sign to her not to speak.

Jean rose quietly, and looked where Randal pointed, and this was what she saw.

She looked over a corner of the old grassy ditch, just where the marsh and the yellow flowers came nearest to it.

Here there stood three tall grey stones, each about as high as a man. Between them, with her back to the single stone, and between the two others facing Randal and Jean, the old nurse was kneeling.

If she had looked up, she could hardly have seen Randal and Jean, for they were within the ditch, and only their eyes were on the level of the rampart.

Besides, she did not look up; she was groping in the breast of her dress for something, and her eyes were on the ground.

'What can the old woman be doing?' whispered Randal. 'Why, she has got my fairy bottle in her hand!'

Then he remembered how he had shown her the bottle, and how she had gone out without giving it back to him.

Jean and he watched, and kept very quiet.

They saw the old nurse, still kneeling, take the stopper out of the black strange bottle, and turn the open mouth gently on her hand. Then she carefully put in the stopper, and rubbed her eyes with the palm of her hand. Then she crawled along in their direction, very slowly, as if she were looking for something in the grass.

Then she stopped, still looking very closely at the grass.

Next she jumped to her feet with a shrill cry, clapping her hands; and then she turned, and was actually *running* along the edge of the marsh, towards Fairnilee.

'Nurse!' shouted Randal, and she stopped suddenly, in a fright, and let the fairy bottle fall.

It struck on a stone, and broke to pieces with a jingling sound, and the few drops of strange water in it ran away into the grass.

'Oh, ma bairns, ma bairns, what have you made me do?'

cried the old nurse pitifully. 'The fairy gift is broken, and maybe the gold of Fairnilee, that my eyes have looked on, will ne'er be seen again.'

Chapter XIII:
THE GOLD OF FAIRNILEE

Randal and Jean went to the old woman and comforted her, though they could not understand what she meant. She cried and sobbed, and threw her arms about; but, by degrees, they found out all the story.

When Randal had told her how all he saw in Fairyland was changed after he had touched his eyes with the water from the bottle, the old woman remembered many tales that she had heard about some charm known to the fairies, which helped them to find things hidden, and to see through walls and stones. Then she had got the bottle from Randal, and had stolen out, meaning to touch her eyes with the water, and try whether *that* was the charm and whether she could find the treasure spoken of in the old rhymes. She went

> *Between the Camp o' Rink*
> *And Tweed-water clear,*

and to the place which lay

> *Atween the wet ground and the dry,*

that is, between the marsh and the Catrail.

Here she had noticed the three great stones, which made a kind of chamber on the hillside, and here she had anointed her eyes with the salt water of the bottle of tears.

Then she had seen through the grass, she declared, and through the upper soil, and she had beheld great quantities of gold. And she was running with the bottle to tell Randal, and to touch his eyes with the water that he might see it also. But, out of Fairyland, the strange water only had its magical power while it was still wet on the eye lashes. This the old nurse soon found; for she went back to the three standing stones, and looked and saw nothing, only grass and daisies. And the fairy bottle was broken, and all the water spilt.

This was her story, and Randal did not know what to believe. But so many strange things had happened to him, that one more did not seem impossible. So he and Jean took the old nurse home, and made her comfortable in her room, and Jean put her to bed, and got her a little wine and an oatcake.

Then Randal very quietly locked the door outside, and put the key in his pocket. It would have been of no use to tell the old nurse to be quiet about what she thought she had seen.

By this time it was late and growing dark. But that night there would be a moon.

After supper, of which there was very little, Lady Ker went to bed. But Randal and Jean slipped out into the moonlight. They took a sack with them, and Randal carried a pickaxe and a spade. They walked quickly to the three great stones, and waited for a while to hear if all was quiet. Then Jean threw a white cloak round her, and stole about the edges of the camp and the wood. She knew that if any wandering man came by, he would not stay long where such a figure was walking. The night was cool, the dew lay on the deep fern; there was a sweet smell from the grass and from the pine-wood.

In the mean time, Randal was digging a long trench with his pickaxe, above the place where the old woman had knelt, as far as he could remember it.

He worked very hard, and when he was in the trench up

to his knees, his pickaxe struck against a stone. He dug round it with the spade, and came to a layer of black burnt ashes of bones. Beneath these, which he scraped away, was the large flat stone on which his pick had struck. It was a wide slab of red sandstone, and Randal soon saw that it was the lid of a great stone coffin, such as the ploughshare sometimes strikes against when men are ploughing the fields in the Border country.

Randal had seen these before, when he was a boy, and he knew that there was never much in them, except ashes and one or two rough pots of burnt clay.

He was much disappointed.

It had seemed as if he was really coming to something, and, behold, it was only an old stone coffin!

However, he worked on till he had cleared the whole of the stone coffin-lid. It was a very large stone chest, and must have been made, Randal thought, for the body of a very big man.

With the point of his pickaxe he raised the lid.

In the moonlight he saw something of a strange shape.

He put down his hand, and pulled it out.

It was an image, in metal, about a foot high, and represented a beautiful woman, with wings on her shoulders, sitting on a wheel.

Randal had never seen an image like this; but in an old book, which belonged to the monks of Melrose, he had seen, when he was a boy, a picture of such a woman.

The monks had told him that she was Dame Fortune, with her swift wings that carry her from one person to another, as luck changes, and with her wheel that she turns with the turning of chance in the world.

The image was very heavy. Randal rubbed some of the dirt and red clay off, and found that the metal was yellow. He cut it with his knife; it was soft. He cleaned a piece, which shone bright and unrusted in the moonlight, and touched it with his tongue. Then he had no doubt any more. The image was *gold*!

Randal now knew that the old nurse had not been mistaken. With the help of the fairy water she had seen *the gold of Fairnilee*. He called very softly to Jeanie, who came glimmering in her white robes through the wood, looking herself like a fairy. He put the image in her hand, and set his finger on his lips to show that she must not speak.

Then he went back to the great stone coffin, and began to grope in it with his hands. There was much earth in it that had slowly sifted through during the many years that it had been buried. But there was also a great round bowl of metal and a square box.

Randal got out the bowl first. It was covered with a green rust, and had a lid; in short, it was a large ancient kettle, such as soldiers use in camp. Randal got the lid off, and, behold, it was all full of very ancient gold coins, not Greek, nor Roman, but like those used in Britain before Julius Caesar came.

The square box was of iron, and was rusted red. On the lid, in the moonlight, Jeanie could read the letters SPQR, but she did not know what they meant. The box had been locked, and chained, and clamped with iron bars. But all was so rusty that the bars were easily broken, and the lid torn off.

Then the moon shone on bars of gold, and on great plates and dishes of gold and silver, marked with letters, and with what Randal thought were crests. Many of the cups were studded with red and green and blue stones. And there were beautiful plates and dishes, purple, gold, and green; and one

192

of these fell, and broke into a thousand pieces, for it was of some strange kind of glass. There were three gold sword-hilts, carved wonderfully into the figures of strange beasts with wings, and heads like lions.

Randal and Jean looked at it and marvelled, and Jean sang in a low, sweet voice:

> *'Between the Camp o' Rink*
> *And Tweed-water clear,*
> *Lie nine kings' ransoms*
> *For nine hundred year!'*

Nobody ever saw so much treasure in all broad Scotland.

Jean and Randal passed the rest of the night in hiding what they had found. Part they hid in the secret chamber of Fairnilee, of which only Jean and Lady Ker and Randal knew. The rest they stowed away in various places. Then Randal filled the earth into the trench, and cast wood on the place, and set fire to the wood, so that next day there was nothing there but ashes and charred earth.

You will not need to be told what Randal did, now that he had treasure in plenty. Some he sold in France, to the king, Henry II, and some in Rome, to the Pope; and with the money which they gave him he bought corn and cattle in England, enough to feed all his neighbours, and stock the farms, and sow the fields for next year. And Fairnilee became a very rich and fortunate house, for Randal married Jean, and soon their children were playing on the banks of the Tweed, and rolling down the grassy slope to the river, to bathe on hot days. And the old nurse lived long and happy among her new bairns, and often she told them how it was *she* who really found the gold of Fairnilee.

You may wonder what the gold was, and how it came there? Probably Father Francis, the good Melrose monk, was right. He said that the iron box and the gold image of Fortune, and the kettle full of coins, had belonged to some regiment of the Roman army: the kettle and the coins they must have taken from the Britons; the box and all the plate were their own, and brought from Italy. Then they, in their turn, must have been defeated by some of the fierce tribes beyond the Roman wall, and must have lost all their treasure. That must have been buried by the victorious enemy; and *they*, again, must have been driven from their strong camp at Rink, either by some foes from the north, or by a new Roman army from the south. So all the gold lay at Fairnilee for many hundred years, never quite forgotten, as the old rhyme showed, but never found till it was discovered, in their sore need, by the old nurse and Randal and Jean.

As for Randal and Jean, they lived to be old, and died on one day, and they are buried at Dryburgh in one tomb, and a green tree grows over them; and the Tweed goes murmuring past their grave, and past the grave of Sir Walter Scott.

Part Five

ENVOY

WHY EVERYONE SHOULD BE ABLE TO TELL A STORY

John Lorne Campbell

Once there was an Uistman who was travelling home, at the time when the passage wasn't as easy as it is today. In those days travellers used to come by the Isle of Skye, crossing the sea from Dunvegan to Lochmaddy. This man had been away working at the harvest on the mainland. He was walking through Skye on his way home, and at nightfall he came to a house, and thought he would stay there till morning, as he had a long way to go. He went in, and I'm sure he was made welcome by the man of the house, who asked him if he had any tales or stories. The Uistman replied that he had never known any.

'It's very strange you can't tell a story,' said his host. 'I'm sure you've heard plenty.'

'I can't remember one,' said the Uistman.

His host himself was telling stories all night, to pass the night, until it was time to go to bed. When they went to bed, the Uistman was given the closet inside the front door to sleep in. What was there hanging in the closet but the carcass of a sheep! The Uistman hadn't been long in bed when he heard the door being opened, and two men came in and took away the sheep.

The Uistman said to himself that it would be very unfortunate for him to let those fellows take the sheep away, for the people of the house would think that he had taken it himself. He went after the thieves, and he had gone some way after them when one of them noticed him, and said to the other:

'Look at that fellow coming after us to betray us; let's go back and catch him and do away with him.'

They turned back, and the Uistman made off as fast as he could to try to get back to the house. But they got between him and the house. The Uistman kept going, until he heard the sound of a big river; then he made for the river. In his panic he went into the river, and the stream took him away. He was likely to be drowned. But he got ahold of a branch of a tree that was growing on the bank of the river, and clung on to it. He was too frightened to move; he heard the two men going back and forth along the banks of the river, throwing stones wherever the trees cast their shade; and the stones were going past him.

He remained there until dawn. It was a frosty night, and when he tried to get out of the river, he couldn't do it. He tried to shout, but he couldn't shout either. At last he managed to utter one shout, and made a leap; and he woke up, and found himself on the floor beside the bed, holding on to the bedclothes with both hands. His host had been casting spells on him during the night! In the morning when they were at breakfast, his host said:

'Well, I'm sure that wherever you are tonight, you'll have a story to tell, though you hadn't one last night.'

That's what happened to the man who couldn't tell a story; everyone should be able to tell a tale or a story to help pass the night!

THE TAIL

J. F. Campbell

There was a shepherd once who went out to the hill to look after his sheep. It was misty and cold, and he had much trouble to find them. At last he had them all but one; and after much searching he found that one too in a peat-hag, half drowned; so he took off his plaid, and bent down and took hold of the sheep's tail, and he pulled! The sheep was heavy with water, and he could not lift her, so he took off his coat and he *pulled*! But it was too much for him, so he spit on his hands, and took a good hold of the tail and he PULLED! And the tail broke! And if it had not been for that this tale would have been a great deal longer.

IRISH FOLK AND FAIRY-TALES
Edited by Gordon Jarvie

There is plenty of mystery and magic in this fascinating collection of Irish fairy-tales, folklore and legends. Much-loved tales include the story of the farmer who offends the fairies by building a house on their dancing ground, the king who loses his wife in a chess game, and the extraordinary adventures of the great Irish hero Cuchulain.

Fairies, phoukas, merrows and leprechauns add to the intrigue and excitement of this well-chosen anthology.

THE LITTLE BOOKROOM
Eleanor Farjeon

When Eleanor Farjeon was a little girl she had one favourite room known as the Little Bookroom, where the overflow of books from all the other rooms was deliciously haphazardly stacked and shelved. That was where she went to read, and 'wander in realms where fancy seemed more true than facts'. No wonder that the Little Bookroom's silver cobwebs clung to the corners of her mind, and that many years later her own books were such a mixture of fiction and fact and fantasy and truth. This collection of her own favourites from all the stories she wrote is a book to be treasured in every family.

A THIEF IN THE VILLAGE
AND OTHER STORIES
James Berry

Wonderfully atmospheric, rich and moving, these very contemporary narratives bring alive the setting and culture highly relevant to today's multi-ethnic Britain.

THE PUFFIN BOOK OF
TWENTIETH CENTURY CHILDREN'S
STORIES

Edited by Judith Elkin

Adventure, fantasy, ghost story, comedy, science fiction, history and fairy-tale – it's all here in an irresistible collection of the best writers for children this century, from Rudyard Kipling to Anne Fine, J. R. R. Tolkien to Betsy Byars, Joan Aiken to Dick King-Smith. Search out old friends and make many more new ones along the way!

ROUGH AND TUMBLE

Edited by Anne Wood and George English

There are ten children in this book – five boys and five girls. BE WARNED! THEY ARE THE WORST CHILDREN EVER! There's Harriet, who takes a crocodile on the school bus; there's Little Alpesh, who demolishes a whole multi-storey car park with his conker; and the terrible Marmalade Atkins, who takes her donkey, Rufus, to the Ritz and causes a riot.

With stories by Dick King-Smith, Roald Dahl, Gene Kemp and Martin Waddell amongst others, there's plenty of fun for everyone.

THE PUFFIN BOOK OF FABULOUS FABLES

Edited by Mark Cohen

What exactly is a fable? What makes it different from an ordinary story? This marvellous collection of fables from all over the world shows you why fables are such special stories, and why they've kept audiences spellbound for centuries. And you can find out how the rhinoceros got his skin, why one swallow doesn't make a summer and what happened to the shepherd boy who cried wolf . . .

THE NEW GOLDEN LAND ANTHOLOGY
Edited by Judith Elkin

Not only traditional stories, tall stories and tongue-twisters, but new stories, nonsense poems and nasty tales, rhymes and riddles, songs and stories of the supernatural make this anthology a treasure trove. A bumper collection for children and adults to share together, with pieces from some of the most talented modern writers for children, including Joan Aiken, Bernard Ashley, Spike Milligan, Roger McGough, Jan Mark and Philippa Pearce.

A NECKLACE OF RAINDROPS
Joan Aiken

Eight beautiful, scintillating, mysterious and magical fantasies which include a home in the sky, a baker's cat who grows huge after eating yeast, a feathered house which lays an egg, a huge flying apple pie with a bit of sky baked into it. With delicious illustrations by Jan Pieńkowski.

I LIKE THIS STORY
Edited by Kaye Webb

In this irresistible and marvellously varied collection, Kaye Webb has unveiled a feast of tantalizing extracts from fifty favourite books. *I Like This Story* will envelop you in fantasy and reality, comedy and drama, from stories famous and not so famous, but all bursting to be devoured and relished. From *Charlotte's Web* to *The BFG*, from *The Borrowers* to *Watership Down*, this absorbing and stimulating selection will transport you into fifty different worlds – and leave you longing for more!

ANOTHER BIG STORY BOOK
Edited by Richard Bamberger

One of the foremost experts on literature for children has collected here some of the world's most enchanting and magical fairy-tales. From the English tale 'Jack and the Beanstalk' to the Indian 'Wali Dad the Simple', these are stories parents will enjoy telling and children will remember with pleasure for the rest of their lives.

BAD BOYS
Edited by Eileen Colwell

All the boys in these twelve stories are bad in one way or another. Either really bad, like Freddie, Adolphus, Edward, Montague, Montmorency and John Henry, who leave their aunts marooned on an island, or only a little bad, like Timothy, who jumps in and out of puddles.

THE *PARENTS* BOOK OF BEDTIME STORIES
Edited by Tony Bradman

Bedtime will always be a pleasure with this refreshing book of bedtime stories drawn from the popular *Parents* magazine. With plenty of lively and appealing characters and a wide range of themes (and all the perfect length for a bedtime slot), this is an ideal addition to the family bookshelf.

THE DOOR IN THE AIR
AND OTHER STORIES
Margaret Mahy

A varied and unusual collection of thought-provoking short stories full of fantasy and magic for the young teenager. An exciting departure for Margaret Mahy, demonstrating her astonishing range.

TEN IN A BED
Allan Ahlberg

An energetic and witty collection of stories about Dinah Price and the surprising visitors she has to entertain. Each night she finds a different fairy-tale character occupying her bed – from Puss in Boots and Sleeping Beauty to a wicked witch and a wolf! They all refuse to budge until Dinah has told them a special bedtime story.

PAST EIGHT O'CLOCK
Joan Aiken

An enchanting collection of stories which are all concerned with sleeping and waking, dreams and bedtime. Each of the eight stories is woven around the theme of a familiar lullaby or bedtime song. Illustrated by the inimitable Jan Pieńkowski.

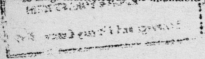